PENGUIN BOOKS

THE HOUSE OF LITTLE SISTERS

Eva Wong Nava was born on a tropical island where a merlion spurts water. Her ancestors braved monsoon winds sailing from the Middle Kingdom to British Malaya to plant roots in Southeast Asia. When the winds changed, her relatives sailed again and found another home somewhere in the western hemisphere, braving snow storms and hail. Eva has done many things in life, like banking and teaching, but writing remains her most favourite thing to do. She combines degrees in literature and art history and writes stories that explore identity, culture, and belonging by adding a dash of magic. Eva has written an award-winning middle-grade book (Moonbeam Children's Book Awards, 2018) and several picture books. She lives in the Land of Albion with her family, two scampering squirrels, and a regal fox. Eva can be found on Twitter, Instagram and Facebook as @evawongnava.

ADVANCE PRAISE FOR
THE HOUSE OF LITTLE SISTERS

'A novel rich in historical detail and memorable characters. Tautly paced and extensively researched.'

—Dave Chua, author of *Gone Case*

'An engrossing read … a testimony of Eva Wong Nava's attention to period details and exquisite storytelling skills'

—Felix Cheong, award-winning author of
Sprawl: A Graphic Novel

'A riveting and masterfully crafted historical fiction.'

—Vivian Teo, author of the *My BFF Is an Alien series*

'A haunting feast for the senses.'

—Daryl Kho, author of *Mist-bound*

'This is an exciting piece of historical fiction anchored by relatable characters, and is the best way to experience the past.'

—Audrey Chin, author of *The Ash House*

'A beautiful, haunting, visceral experience. You'll savour the sights, sounds and smells of pre-WW II Singapore and be mesmerized by a cast of characters as delicately layered and sumptuously rich as a delicious kueh lapis. If this book were a dish, it would deserve five Michelin Stars. Eva Wong-Nava cooks up a special tale that will be savoured by generations to come.'

—Dave Seow, children's book author of
more than 45 books

'In this fresh and richly-detailed YA historical novel, Eva Wong Nava helps to expose Western readers, in particular, to the culture of 1930s British Malaya, exposing new audiences not only to words like Peranakan and Pontianak, but to the plight of the young mui tsai sold as indentured servants into homes like that of "Number One Madam", where they must struggle against the prevailing norms to find any semblance of happiness, contentment, or sense of identity.'

—E.S. Alexander, award-winning non-fiction writer and author of historical novel, *Lies That Blind*

'This is the most flavourful book! First we are served mouth-watering Nyonya dishes, but then the taste turns bitter. Bitter like the Chinese medicine girls sip to stem a bleed. *The House of Little Sisters* brings to life an often forgotten time, a time were little girls were sold to work in the big houses of rich Peranakan families. They face rape, exploitation, and loneliness. Thankfully, Eva Wong Nava also shows us love, hope, and change in the air for girls like Mei Mei. This book is an eye-opening window into the lives of Singapore's mui tsai, that I highly recommend to teenagers and their parents alike.'

—Karien van Ditzhuijzen, author of *A Yellow House*

'Riveting and impossible to put down! Such a beautiful, exciting, bittersweet story of old Nanyang that is suffused with longing and nostalgia. The cast of characters come alive through Eva's masterful storytelling, and we see the story unfold through their eyes like a waking dream. Absolutely loved it!'

—Sim Ee Waun, author of *The House on Silat Road &* *The House on Palmer Road*

The House of Little Sisters

Eva Wong Nava

PENGUIN BOOKS
An imprint of Penguin Random House

PENGUIN BOOKS

USA | Canada | UK | Ireland | Australia
New Zealand | India | South Africa | China | Southeast Asia

Penguin Books is part of the Penguin Random House group of companies
whose addresses can be found at global.penguinrandomhouse.com

Published by Penguin Random House SEA Pte Ltd
9, Changi South Street 3, Level 08-01,
Singapore 486361

First published in Penguin Books by Penguin Random House SEA 2022
Copyright © Eva Wong Nava 2022

ISBN 9789814882279

Printed at Markono Print Media Pte Ltd, Singapore
Typeset in Garamond by MAP Systems, Bangalore, India

www.penguin.sg

To Nora, who believed in this project.
To my family, past, present, and future—I leave you this legacy.

'You may choose to look the other way but you can never say again that you did not know.'—William Wilberforce, British politician and abolitionist

'Human rights are not a privilege conferred by government. They are every human being's entitlement by virtue of his humanity.'—Mother Teresa, saint and missionary

'And though she be but little she is fierce!'—William Shakespeare (from *A Midsummer Night's Dream*)

Contents

Preface

It is said that in a land known as British Malaya, where monsoon winds blow and the air is hot and humid, legends and folklore abound. They were brought to this land by travellers and seafarers who must become masters, servants and merchants, and wear a new skin known to their descendants as diaspora.

It is known that ghosts and spirits live amongst the people of this land, that their powerful essences and energies both inspire and frighten the living. Rituals and prayers are proffered to the inhabitants of the other realm to keep them there so that the lives of the living remain harmonious.

Once a year, the gates of Hell fling open to let these inhabitants out for a month-long jaunt amongst the living. It is known that some spirits cannot be appeased and they must be left alone to roam the earth, raging and forever seeking to be consoled. These spirits are best left to their own devices for there is no comforting them, and if you see one, you must flee. But when the spirits start to speak, you must listen. They bring with them tales of woe laced with desire; stories that ask to be remembered by the living and to be repeated for time immemorial lest we forget them.

This is a sad tale of the fate of little girls, mui tsai, who are both powerful and helpless. Their stories need to be heard and shared.

It is also a story of forbidden love, magic, and faith: A story of two young lovers who must find their place on earth to be together.

Let us begin this tale of love, longing, and lust.

That I want Thee, only thee—let my heart repeat without end.
All desires that distract me, day and night,
are false and empty to the core.
As the night keeps hidden in its gloom the petition for light,
even thus in the depth of my unconsciousness rings the cry—
'I want thee, only thee'
As the storm still seeks its end in peace when it strikes against
peace with all its might, even thus my rebellion strikes against thy love
and still its cry is—'I want thee, only thee'.

—Rabindranath Tagore

Cast of Characters

- Lim Mei Mei/Ah Mei/Mei
- Ah Wan Jie/Kakak Wan
- Hassan Mohamed
- Encik Mohammad Abdullah/ Pak Abdullah
- Ah Lian
- Ah Poh
- Ah Ping Yee/Ping-chieh
- Ah Choo
- Ah Mooi
- Ah Chin
- Precious Jade/Po Gek/Ah Yoke
- Master Lee/Percival Lee Book Tong/Percy Lee
- Eminent Mister Lee/Lee Guang Hoe
- Number One Madam
- New Number Two Madam
- Tang Siu Lan
- Mr Tang/Mr Tang Yong Ban & Mrs Tang
- Mr & Mrs Chew
- Mrs Shirin Fozdar

- Mrs Elizabeth Smith
- Mrs Wu
- Man with glass/cloudy eye
- Mister Pickering
- Ban Guan, the messenger boy
- Ching/Ma
- Ah Pa/Ah Leong
- Huat/Ah Huat
- Ah Mah
- Uncle Cheong
- Aunty Eng

'Ah', a prefix 阿 (ā) used by the Chinese to address children or people considered diminutive. It is also used as a prefix attached to the name of a loved one; a prefix of endearment. In the Chinese language, Ah has no meaning. It is both an endearing and infantilizing manner of reference.

Chapter 1

Singapore Town, The Lee Household, August 1931

It is the evening before the full moon in the seventh lunar month. Not long after we lost Ah Lian. Ah Mei arrives, brought into the kitchen by Ah Chin, just as I am finishing folding the last of the gold ingots.

'The new *mui tsai*,' Ah Chin says, 'Ban Guan just dropped her off.'

I nod in acknowledgement and send him on his way. Ah Chin has aged, his back now a little stooped and his gait tells me that his left hip is giving him problems again. The light in the kitchen is dim, but there is enough to make out the form of the mui tsai.

I gesture for the new girl to come closer with both my hands. 'Come, come.'

A pressing rheumatoid ache creeps from my wrists to my fingers as they fold and unfold moving with my gesture. My right hand worse than my left.

1

I feel her energy within the circle of space between us. The girl's presence is strong. There is something about Mei that speaks to me. She is polite, greeting me with the honorific, Aunty, which shows that she is well brought up, though there is a streak in her that needs to be reined in. A nagging sensation rattles my old bones.

'Welcome to the Lee family home. What is your name?'

'Lim Mei Mei, Aunty.' The timbre of her voice is low, filled with yang energy.

'Ah, a Fukien name. Your father was from the Fujian province?'

'Yes, Aunty.' She looks at me, holding my gaze for a few seconds. Unlike Ah Lian, Mei's dark eyes shine with intelligence under a pair of perfectly arched eyebrows. Her heart-shaped face is kind. A striking face, no doubt, accentuated by her prominent widow's peak. What do they say about a widow's peak? Was it that such girls are alluring and mysterious? Or was it that they're sexually charged? Whatever it is they say, I shall find out soon enough.

'How old are you, Mei?'

'Sixteen. My birthday was yesterday.'

She is a waif of a girl. Small for her sixteen years. A little too old for the job she's been brought in to do, I am thinking. Her job, I'm sure, is to look after Ah Yoke mainly, just like what Ah Lian was tasked to do. May her spirit rest in peace. By force of habit, I rub the amulet pinned to my collar as I recall the memory of Ah Lian.

Ah Mei has come with a bundle of clothes and a pair of *kasut manik* on her feet. I know that those beaded slippers don't belong to her. She must have been given them. They are tatty and many of the glass beads making up a pattern of peonies are missing. Cast offs because a girl like Mei would never be in possession of such beautiful footwear.

'Did you make those?'

'No, Aunty,' Mei answers quietly, 'they were my mother's—she was given them by the lady she works for.'

'Best put them away because you won't be needing them anymore. Wait here. I have something for you.'

I go to fetch the pair of canvas shoes that Number One Madam had told me the night before to give to the new girl when she arrives. They were Ah Lian's and she had only worn them a couple of times. The canvas shoes have been packed away with some of Ah Lian's old things. I've kept them in my cupboard in the room that I used to share with her. I was only instructed to give the new girl Ah Lian's old shoes. Number One Madam did not leave more instructions other than this. Kept with the shoes is a set of Ah Lian's *samfoo* which I'd washed and folded away, but I don't suppose it would fit Mei. She's a lot smaller and thinner than Ah Lian. I have also kept the bar of soap that belonged to Ah Lian, a pair of wooden clogs, and an old sarong for the new girl to use. I pick the canvas shoes, clogs, sarong, and soap up with a sigh and give them to their new owner.

The new mui tsai accepts the hand-me-downs humbly, taking them from me with a nod of gratitude and a soft thank you. I find Ah Mei to be obedient and gentle in her manners. This is usually the way when a girl does not know her own beauty or her own worth.

Along with the beaded slippers, the girl is wearing a samfoo that no doubt is not hers either. The cotton is of good quality and the buttons are well sewn. The trousers are frayed at the hem, mended a few times, from the look of them. The blouse is stained under the armpits.

'Did you make that samfoo?'

'No, Aunty! This was what Mother's Madam had given her for me. All I did was sew on the press studs ... and ... and ... mended the trouser legs.'

Mei has some talent there judging from the way the stitches look. Perhaps, Ah Lian's old samfoo would come into good use after Mei is done taking the blouse in; the pants would be too short though, but some people just don't have the luxury of choice. My thoughts are interrupted by something around Ah Mei's neck—her necklace. The chain is of gold and the pendant a gleaming jade Guanyin. The jade looks to be of good quality too.

'Where did you get that necklace, girl?'

'My Ma, Aunty. She gave it to me for protection and made me promise to always wear it.'

As she says this, I swear the jade Goddess starts to shimmer in the last light of the day.

I have to look away. The pendant's energy is gripping.

Ah Mei must have travelled a long way because her feet are caked in dirt and blisters, and she smells of old laundry.

'Go bathe in the outhouse. Wear these pair of wooden clogs,' I tell her immediately, wanting to be left alone to eat my dinner, the leftovers from the day's party food.

Mei looks at me bewildered. 'Outhouse, Aunty?'

'You don't know what an outhouse is?' I ask Mei, perhaps a little too gruffly.

She shrinks at the tone of my voice and shakes her head. The hunger is making me irritable, so I think it is best to leave the last preparations for tomorrow's rituals and all that I had to do with the girl until later.

'Let's eat first. Then I will show you everything.'

It has been a long day. Number One Madam had been entertaining all afternoon. She had invited her clan sisters, wives of wealthy men like her, to dine and gamble. It was a session of *mahjong* today. Last week, it was *cherki*, a card game similar to mahjong. She wanted to serve her sisters *laksa* for breakfast and chicken curry with white rice for lunch, with a spicy cucumber salad. For dessert, she had ordered a *kueh lapis* and *chendol* for tea before their last round. Layered cakes like the lapis are labour intensive. Luckily, their gambling sessions can go on for a bit, which gives me time to grate the coconut to make the milk for the chendol. As for the cake, I baked it the day before. So, as you can imagine, I am bone tired after cooking all day for two days and then serving the guests who have finally all left. All I want to do now is to eat and go to bed. In the morning, I have some other things to take care of. The thirty-day rituals and prayers for the Month of the Hungry Ghost would begin tomorrow and I have a lot to do. Not only that, there is still the day's food to prepare.

Mei stands there not knowing what to do. I am sure she must be starving.

'Thank you, Aunty. Please tell me what you'd like me to cook.'

I can't help but laugh and immediately, Mei's complexion turns crimson.

'I'm the cook, Mei! You're here to do something else.'

I am surprised that she doesn't know her role. But then, thinking more about it, how could she? I can only imagine that she was taken in a hurry from her home, like all the many mui tsai sold to rich families like the Lees as servant girls. Ah Lian had come in a similar way.

Lim Mei Mei no doubt was bought to look after the Lee daughter, Precious Jade or Po Gek in Fukien. I call her Ah Yoke since I am Cantonese. But never in front of Number One Madam. Ah Yoke is always Elder Daughter in front of Madam. I must make sure that the new mui tsai knows this too. But hungry stomachs must be satiated first.

'There's plenty of food left. All spicy … food, you'll see, we have plenty in this house.'

We are about to start on our dinner when Number One Madam's servant girl comes into the kitchen to inform me that the Madam wants a word with me. I leave reluctantly for the main house. The kitchen and the servants' quarters are joined to the main part of the house by a long internal corridor. When Mother was the cook, the walkway was outside and she had to serve the food at the mercy of the weather. Not easy to ferry clay pots of curries and stews, and small dishes of snacks in the monsoon rain, I tell you. It was Eminent Mister Lee's father who'd suggested enclosing the walkway within two walls and a tiled roof. He was such a kind-hearted man. Pity his son turned out the opposite way. I hobble up the grand stairs to the dining room, my arthritic knees creaking with a dull ache. Number One Madam is seated on a rosewood chair by the side table, where tea and cakes are served to friends and family, waiting for me.

'Hah, Wan Jie, good, you're here.' Number One Madam's voice is authoritative as always. I suppose a lady of her status must command respect. She is younger than me, but already has the air of an older woman. It must come from being married to a wealthy man, almost the same age as her father. In the shadow, Number One Madam looks almost ethereal, ghost-like even. She is sitting upright, at the edge of the seat, her right-hand cupping and encircling her left fist.

A brooding sadness hangs in the air.

'A new mui tsai has arrived. She is to look after our Precious Jade, Po Gek.'

Number One Madam pauses and looks at me, studying my face. Waiting for a reaction, no doubt. But I do not betray my feelings.

'Yes, Madam. She is in the kitchen now, waiting.'

'Good, good, I want you to be in charge of her as usual. Her only role is to take care of Po Gek, and you need to show the new mui tsai the ropes, since our Precious Jade spends so much time in the kitchen.'

I nod.

'And ... '

'Yes, Madam ... '

'Perhaps Po Gek need not spend so much time in the kitchen. What good is it for her to be there so much?' After she says this, Number One Madam looks away from me and lowers her eyes to look at her hands, folded on her lap.

'If you so wish, Madam.'

'And ... ' she looks up from staring at her folded hands.

'Yes, Madam.'

'With the new mui tsai ... ' her voice trails off as if she is thinking about something more important than what she has already instructed me to do, '... let her take Po Gek to the market and for walks.'

'If that is your wish, Madam.'

I wonder what has made Number One Madam change her mind. The Lee daughter should be forbidden to leave the house. What will people think? I have nothing to be ashamed of here. My face although not a pretty sight because of a red berry-like stain across my left cheek isn't as bad as Ah Yoke's split lip. And, I am the daughter of an unimportant servant. Of course I don't let on how I really feel. In fact, I am relieved that Ah Yoke and her mui tsai would be out of my hair soon.

Number One Madam shifts in her seat. Then, after clearing her throat, she says, 'What I want to say is really this ... you know what it is, don't you?'

'What is it, Madam?' I reply cautiously, '... what is it that you want to instruct me?'

'... Ah Wan Jie, you know what I mean,' she answers, her voice quiet, equally cautious, '... the same rules apply.'

I nod again, swallowing hard.

I wait for her to dismiss me but nothing. The shadows of leaves imprinted on the wall move with the flickering flame of the only candle in the room. My stomach is growling so hard I can hear it in my head. I hope I don't have to apply the same rules like I had to for Ah Lian. I feel that it's not really my responsibility and I resent it that Number One Madam has laid this on my shoulders again. But my heart softens just looking at her sitting there, scared and lonely, even if she can be menacing.

'How does she look?' her voice cracks as she whispers this.

'Ordinary.'

In the shadows, I see Number One Madam nodding her head as she gets up from her seat.

I back away to make space for her to walk past. She brushes past me with her head held high.

'Remember ... same rules apply,' she says without turning back, the scent of rose water trailing after her.

Chapter 2

Ah Mei is still standing in the same spot where I had left her.

'Come, let's eat,' I say gently.

'Thank you, Aunty.'

'You can call me Ah Wan Jie, like all the mui tsai and Number One Madam. Better that I am sister to you than Aunty. But never be mistaken that we are the same, you understand?'

'Yes, Ah Wan Jie.'

'After, I will show you what to do. You need a wash, you stink.'

I notice that Ah Mei eats slowly, chewing her food with care. A good sign because it shows that she is not greedy. Perhaps it is the heat of the curries that she's not used to. I can only imagine this being a possibility for someone coming from the countryside. Ah Mei is ethnic Chinese and the Lees are Peranakan, children of the soil, though they have retained many of our ancient Chinese customs. The Peranakan-Chinese cuisine does not suit everyone, especially us ethnic Chinese. After so many decades in this household, there are still some curries that cause my body to heat up and sweat. The curry was left over from the mahjong luncheon party; the coconut sauce hasn't soured, which makes it still edible. Mei seems to be thinking about something as she chews on her food. She doesn't gobble down her meal, like Ah Lian had, always reaching out for seconds or thirds. Mei eats the portion she has been given and doesn't ask for more. She seems to know her boundaries.

'Where do we wash the dishes, Aunty?' Ah Mei asks as she collects them when I have finished.

'Ah Wan Jie.'

'Of course, I must remember … it is Ah Wan Jie.'

I show her to the air well, where we keep two large ceramic jars to collect rain water. Above the air well is the sky. It's the only part of the house exposed to the elements. The air well is where we wash our vegetables, meat, and dirty dishes. On rainy days, we do our washing under the eaves to stay dry. I watch Ah Mei as she washes up. I notice how meticulous she is. She even looks into the teacups before chucking the remains out and washing them thoroughly in the soapy water. She dries the crockery with a dish cloth hanging on the wall. The girl has initiative. She should have asked first, of course, but it is a good sign, though I know that one step out of bounds, she will end up in the wrong place. I make a mental note to speak to her about this.

After she has stowed away the crockery used only by the servants, Mei stands waiting for me to instruct her on what to do next. Number One Madam has a list of things that I must do with all new mui tsai entering the Lee gate.

'Follow me.' I take her to her bedroom, which she will share with me. Number One Madam has since changed the sleeping arrangements after what had happened with Ah Lian. The room is big enough and rules are rules.

'Here is your bed. You can put away your things in the drawer there.'

'Yes, Ah Wan Jie. Thank you.'

She doesn't have a lot, which is quite normal. They never come with many things. And they won't leave with much either if they can leave at all. Let's see if Number One Madam finds her a good husband in a couple years.

'Take your top and bottom off,' I command Ah Mei, 'there are things that need to be looked at first before you take your bath.'

'What? But—'

'Are you disobeying my orders, young girl?' I say with authority. 'Let me tell you this, as long as you're in my kitchen and under my care, I am in charge.'

With this, Ah Mei strips off her blouse. A sour odour hits my nose, it reaches me from her underarms, and I hold my breath as I examine her. She has a good amount of hair peeking from her armpits, a sign that she is fertile. Her breasts are ample enough, they are at the size they're already at, I think to myself, and apart from some scars from mosquito stings, there are no signs of scurvy or skin disease. Number One Madam has a thing about bad skin. She sacked a mui tsai because the poor girl had bad eczema and was always scratching and sloughing skin. I don't know where this poor girl ended up because the Lees had paid quite a bit of money for her, I was told. I think that Number One Madam had brokered a deal with a brothel in the city and she was sold to them. May the Mother Guanyin Goddess keep her safe. May the Goddess also protect the many mui tsai in this wretched world.

After I have examined her upper body, Mei then takes her lower garments off and lies on the ground like I asked her to. It's not easy for me in this position, kneeling down on my swollen knees, but I won't have her lying on the bed. The girl has not washed for days. A musty smell emanates from between her legs but she looks fine down there. She resists me when I push her legs apart, which is always a good sign. You'd be surprised how many mui tsai will open their legs without resisting. This always tells me that they know what to do. I part the flesh at her crotch. Ah Mei is a virgin and she is also clean below, no mangy blisters or pubic lice that I can see hiding in the triangular jungle between her legs.

'Sit up,' I say, so I can check her head for nits. It doesn't matter if a girl is okay down there, you won't believe how many of these mui tsai come with a head full of lice and eggs.

That is when I catch sight of her unusual mole. I shiver despite the hot humid night.

There is a saying amongst us Malayans. A saying that Mother told me once a long time ago. One mustn't wake the Pontianak—the ancestral spirit of the indigenous Malays—by unhinging the screw at the back of her nape. The Pontianak is a woman who has lost her baby and she is raging in longing for her stillborn child. She has an anger so raw that she will slash you with her claws and eat your heart while it is still beating and your last breath is still warm.

The mole on Ah Mei's neck must not be removed. This is a rule.

Chapter 3

I can't begin to explain the embarrassment that Ah Wan Jie put me through. Even Ma has never touched me this way before. What was that all about? She made me feel so dirty, so impure. I am glad for some time alone at the outhouse. At least there is some sort of a room to have a bath in.

The outhouse is a tiny wood shack with a cement floor. A pipe, connected to a tap, runs into the outhouse from outside through a hole by the metal door. A Shanghai jar, severely cracked at the rim stands below the dripping tap. It's filled with water and a rusty tin bucket for bathing floats in it. I start by washing between my legs to remove the touch of Ah Wan Jie's prying fingers. I watch the soapy water drain away through the plug hole under my parted legs. A pair of whiskers peek from the hole, twitching. A cockroach is trying to escape. There's nothing worse than a flying cockroach and I must stop it quickly. I remove one clog, squat down and strike the plug hole with it, smashing the menacing beast to a pulp. My bare foot is now resting on the wet cement floor while I wash the dead cockroach away with a bucketful of water. As much as I hate the feeling of the damp rough floor, I am eager to scrub the grime off my feet. I take the other clog off and squat once more so I can wash my feet properly. Some blisters have burst and my feet smart when I rub the soap over them. Done with my feet, I start on my hair. Still squatting, I bend my head and feel inside the Shanghai jar for the bucket. I find it and throw a scoop of cold water on my head. My body reacts by shivering. By the third scoop, I'm fine. It is a relief to be able to give my head a good wash and to pour buckets of water over myself without worrying about rationing. After I've washed away all the soapy residue, I put the piece of soap back into the plastic box it came from. For the second time, I am thankful for a room to wash in: taking a bath in the privacy of an outhouse is a luxury compared to bathing by a public pump. Ah, it feels so good to be all scrubbed up and smelling like a fresh flower. Jasmine—I think the soap is scented with. I know the smell because we have a jasmine plant growing wild in our backyard. Its tiny white flowers are delicate and pure, and their sweet scent is most prominent in the morning.

The yard of printed cloth, a sarong as Ah Wan Jie had called it, makes a good flannel for drying. I think she meant for me to use it this way, but frankly, now that I'm all dry, I don't really know what else to do with this piece of cloth. I wonder if I should wrap my wet hair with it. On my way to the Lee house, I did see some women wearing them like skirts as they made their way out of some very big mansions, though they had on a blouse with theirs. Ah Wan Jie didn't give me one. Should I put my sweaty samfoo top back on and wear the sarong like a skirt? I'm not keen to wear my smelly top now that I'm all perfumed with jasmine. Perhaps I need to wrap this skirt around me. That is what I must do, I finally decide. I step into the sarong tube and bring it up to my chest. It hangs off me and to make it stay on, I clutch the cloth to my chest. No, this won't do as I need my hands. I have to find a way to tighten the sarong around my chest. I fiddle with it, not sure what to do best. I try tying it by making a knot at the front, but as soon as I let my hands go, the cloth falls to my ankles. I pick it up and start again. Finally, I pinch and fold the cloth under my right armpit and then roll the folds down twice so the sarong will stay on me. I think I've got it because when I raise my arms up, the sarong doesn't fall down. I got the idea from a Malay aunty in our *kampung*. I'd seen how Emak Amina wears her sarong after her bath at the communal pump. She told me that a sarong and a long blouse are to Malay women what a samfoo is to us Chinese. It doesn't matter that I am missing a blouse, I have to work with what I've got. When I'm certain that the sarong will not fall, I pick up my dirty bundle of clothes hanging on a nail in the wall and step into the wooden clogs again. The clogs are for me to go to the outhouse and back with, Ah Wan Jie had said. I take a couple of small steps, constricted by the tubular skirt, towards the rusty metal door. It's not easy clad in a sarong and walking in a pair of clogs too big for me.

The door creaks as I push it open. I clutch my samfoo to my chest and I take a step over the threshold, holding on the door jamb for balance. Then my right foot catches on the raised plank and I stumble and trip, leaving one clog behind, and scattering my bundle of clothes on the wet dirt floor. Blast! I pick myself up and dust the sand from my palms. While bending down to collect my damp samfoo, I catch a flicker of a shadow from the corner of my eye. Shuddering, I try as best as I can to keep calm. After I've found the missing clog, I take hurried but small steps towards the house, following the path towards the light in the distance. The path to the outhouse is surrounded by shrubs and bushes. A frangipani tree stands sentry by the brick bathroom, its flowers perfuming the still air. The moon is the only sliver of light from behind the tree.

The ghosts don't come out until tomorrow. I know this because Ah Mah had said this morning that the day of my departure was fine since the Hungry Ghost Month won't begin until the next day. I saw the joss sticks and paper ingots that Ah Wan Jie had prepared piled up on the dinner table, ready for tomorrow's sacrificial ritual. I keep on walking towards the house, eyes ahead. The crickets are making a racket. This is mixed with the echoes of monkeys shrieking in the distance. The wooden clogs click on the path as I walk. Somehow, it is a comforting sound against the chirping of the crickets and the strange shrieks and chatter beyond the Lee compound. My jade Guanyin will protect me and I give her a little rub for good measure. She is slightly hot to the touch.

A wisp of a breeze rustles up some dried leaves, and I feel something inside me move. There's a voice in my head and it transports me to another world.

The night air is chilly, Mei. I feel the prickles of goosebumps on my translucent skin. Do you feel them too? Vapours of jasmine, sandalwood, smokey musk. Hmm, the plumes of incense smoke wafting in the air; you know why they're there, Mei—the spirits need a path home. The smoke is there to show me the way back, but it is not time for me to come home yet. The smoke is strong in my memory. It must be strong in yours too. Do you remember the nights during the Hungry Ghost Festival when you used to light joss sticks for your Ah Gong and Tua Ko? The hungry ghosts, like your two relatives, must follow the smoke trail to get home, where they'll imbibe the fragrance of the food left out for them. This is how I must eat now too.

I am ravenous, Mei. It hasn't been long since I inhabited this world. Not long, yet I feel that I've been here for a long time, a ghost floating in and out, living between two worlds.

We are all ghosts, always hungry for something bigger than ourselves, something larger than the taste of the first thing that our lips had touched. That first kiss can be so addictive that our bodies may forget but our spirit does not let go. I would never have known the feeling of such hunger if like you, I'd stayed with my family. But like you, I had no choice. I'm telling you: you must cling to the memory of your mother, Huat and Ah Mah, the three of them existing in that small flat behind the speckled red door. You will always be hungry, hungry for their touch and their love. This hunger cannot be satiated with fires and offerings.

I am raging for it all to end but fate can be both benevolent and cruel. You will know what I mean soon, Mei.

Do not be afraid, Mei. I am not harmful, just starving. I hunger for your company and yearn for the years of lost love and friendship, a longing that only you can fill. Come walk with me. Remember this path ... you must remember ...

... let's walk along this dirt road, past the local mosque. Remember? Veer a little left and you'll see a shanty town of houses with corrugated roofs, scattered here and there. Walk further along and you'll soon come to an almost derelict building that seems uninhabited. It is only when night falls that you'll see four or five lit windows and other signs that people live there. Look harder, don't forget ... remember.

When the wind blows in the right direction, whiffs of savoury ginger and garlic hang in the air ... sniff the air. A line of laundry tells you that there is piped water again. A pump by the road is the source for the water. Once, a man had a dream of building a block of homes for the people in this small village. But he had long ago abandoned his project because he'd run out of money. The rent is cheap and the folks who live there don't mind the grey mouldy walls and sharing their homes with stray cats and dogs, some chickens scratching for worms, and the odd mynah nesting in the rafters. You lived here, Mei ... remember.

As you enter the building, walk up two flights of stairs and along the corridor, you'll soon come to a red door at the end. See the missing flecks of red exposing the natural wood underneath? Gently push this red door open and inside you'll see a simple living room with a threadbare sofa, a single bed and a little kitchen where wholesome meals are cooked. A man's shirt hangs on a peg near the main door, a shirt that has not been worn for many years.

Right above the threadbare sofa is a wooden shelf. There, you'll see an altar inhabited by Guanyin, the Goddess of Mercy and an ancestral tablet, where the soul of the family patriarch resides. It is for this soul that you toss money to be burnt and put food out for him to consume … remember … and don't forget … the two women, a little girl and her brother, the inhabitants of this little flat. The younger woman, the mother, is a gastronomic magician. The older, the grandmother, has a frozen shoulder and a love for the Goddess so profound that she can be heard muttering prayers and clicking her prayer beads all day. The young girl, an angel with intense eyes, sees patterns in tea leaves and talks to the stars—that's you. Don't forget her. The little boy with the unusual toes, will give you the brightest grin, if you tousle his mop of hair.

Take it all in … remember them … and don't forget how you were wrenched from the people you love and who loved you. And, remember too, do not let the Lee household get away with it. Rage, rage, rage against this injustice.

* * *

'Ah Mei! Ah Mei!' Someone is shaking me, calling my name, pulling me back. When my vision clears, I see a terrified Ah Wan Jie and feel her tapping my cheeks urgently. I am in the kitchen once more. I don't know how I got here.

'What are you doing, Ah Mei?' she asks, her voice is strung with agitation, 'you were mumbling about two women and some men … something to do with a little girl and her brother … and raging, raging—'

'Sorry, Ah Wan Jie, I don't know what you're talking about.' I feel dazed and discombobulated.

'Ah Mei, don't scare me, ha!' she says and then drops her voice, 'tomorrow is Ghost Month and I haven't blessed the house yet. I was going to and then you showed up. And then Number One Madam wanted a word and I got distracted. Maybe I should pray now that you acted like a spirit had disturbed you.'

'I am fine—' I want to tell her something about the flicker that I saw earlier but Ah Wan Jie doesn't let me finish my thoughts. She goes to the altar in the corner of the kitchen and lights a joss stick. I know that this is the Kitchen God because we have one too in our humble home.

'Protect me, oh Pu Sat, protect me. I only did what I had to do, bless her soul, Pu Sat, bless her soul. Tomorrow I will burn for her money and cook her all the things she likes to eat. Please protect me Pu Sat,' she chants in loud whispers as she moves the joss stick held between her palms from her forehead towards the altar and back, her body swaying and bending to some ectoplasmic rhythm.

Ah Wan Jie kneels and touches her forehead to the floor while raising her palms, still joined flat holding the incense stick, high above her head. She peels herself off the ground, leaning on one elbow to stand up. She wobbles as if she is about to fall and I lurch forward to catch her. She nods curtly and then plants the joss stick into an urn and bows her head three times, each bow accompanied by a whisper of something I don't understand.

She reaches for a bowl of water on a small wooden table below the Kitchen God's altar. Ah Wan Jie's voice quivers as she continues to mutter sprinkling some water around herself, spraying droplets around the kitchen and raining some down on me. I have never seen so much obeisance being paid to the

Jade Emperor through his messenger before, and it isn't even anywhere near the Chinese New Year. Not even Ah Mah, who loves the Guanyin Goddess so much has prayed the way Ah Wan Jie is doing now.

My necklace sears and I feel a dull ache at my temples and behind my head at the base of my neck.

'Let's get ready for bed now,' Ah Wan Jie says, turning to me after her frenzied prayers.

Chapter 4

The room is small but large enough to have two single beds at each corner. Our beds are separated by an old dresser. Sitting on the dresser top is the Mother Goddess Guanyin. A small vase with a stalk of chrysanthemum accompanies her along with a dish of two oranges and a bunch of bananas. Pinned on the wall to the right of the Goddess is a painting of a phoenix. It resembles a dancing red and yellow flame. The bird's head is in profile and it is wearing a crown of feathers. I fix my eyes on the image, mesmerized by its powerful plumage. The phoenix flaps its wings and turns to look at me. Its eyes glow with wisdom.

'The *fenghuang*, Mei. I see you're as charmed by it as I am,' Ah Wan Jie says breaking the trance. 'It is a symbol of *yin* and *yang*, reminding us that we are made of both male and female essences.'

I gulp in response. The walls are rippling.

'Yin-yang—it's the balance that counts,' she continues. Then she says, pointing to the bottom drawer of the dresser, 'You'll find new sets of samfoo there.'

As soon as I've put on a fresh set of clothes, I start to feel giddy again. A throbbing ache spreads from my shoulders to my chest and I feel out of breath. The voice in my head is whispering once more. I do not recognize this voice, yet this voice knows me, knows Huat, Ma and Ah Mah. Aching with a dizzy sense of déjà vu, and the gnawing pain of knowing that I may never see my family again, I lie down. I am exhausted. As soon as I rest my head on the flat pillow, I fall into a deep sleep.

In my dream that night, I am walking on the dirt path that takes me home. It's at the end of a long pebbly road surrounded by jungle. I see the houses scattered higgledy-piggledy just before I come to the shanty town of low buildings, where our flat is. I am folding Hell money into ingots and throwing them into the pyre. The flames from the pyre look like dancing phoenixes.

* * *

I wake the next morning to a cockerel crowing. The remnants from my dream melt away as my eyes adjust to the semi-darkness. I am disoriented for a few seconds. A window with a thin curtain by my bed tells me that I'm not at home. I remember where I am. I sit up and reach over to pull the curtains apart and push the window open letting in the crisp morning air. The night is beginning to turn into day. Ah Wan Jie's bed is empty. I don't know what I am meant to do. I guess I have to find Ah Wan Jie in the kitchen.

The kitchen is quiet. By habit, I bow before the kitchen altar. There are lit incense sticks stuck into a joss bowl already offered to the Kitchen God. A coil of incense hangs by the altar. I look around the space and see plates of ghost cakes—*mantou* buns dusted with a pink dye—on the servant's dining table. Ah Wan Jie had also prepared some peanut candy. On a red plastic plate, there is a bunch of bananas and a whole papaya resting in another. In a tin tray are three bowls of rice, three cups of brown liquid, tea or maybe brandy, and a boiled chicken perched on a dish. This is way more ghost food than I am used to.

I don't see Ah Wan Jie but I hear clanging coming from outside the kitchen.

'Ah, good, you're awake,' Ah Wan Jie says, on entering the kitchen, 'help me take those platters to the back garden. We will burn money first.' She is holding three red candles and a packet of joss sticks. 'Take that bag of ingots with you as well.'

'Yes, Ah Wan Jie.'

I know what the mantou buns and candy are for. They're for the hungry souls of children who have died tragically. Ma used to put them out for her lost babies. Aunty Li in our kampung had done the same.

Before moving to the shanty town, we used to live in a kampung, in a village, where houses on stilts with thatched roofs stood. When it rained, rivers of yellow would flow below our wooden hut, gushing and rushing to meet other streams of yellow joining the canals and rivers. If the roof needed mending, water seeped through. Thatching was not something that I could do nor could Ma and Ah Mah. Ah Mah is too old and can't use her arms any longer. She used to hoe the paddy fields behind our thatched house, planting green vegetables, sweet potatoes, and onions. But that was taken away from us when we couldn't pay the rent anymore. Ah Pa didn't send money home and hadn't for months on end when the land owner took all our food and told us that he was giving the field away to another family. The family was kind and would give us some of their vegetables, ones that they couldn't sell at the market, from time to time.

Little fires were found everywhere in our small kampung. During funerals, paper houses and paper clothes and shoes, sometimes paper effigies representing the sons that the deceased couldn't have or the spouses that they couldn't marry, would be burnt at the sacrificial pyre to the dead. The biggest bonfire was always on the Feast of the Hungry Ghost. During the Month of Ghosts, Chinese neighbours would light incense and burn paper money to appease the lost souls, hungry ghosts, that cannot be satiated. And on the fifteenth day of this month—the seventh lunar month—a feast would be prepared as these souls were let out of Hell, ravenous. They haven't eaten for a whole year, and are only allowed to roam our world once a year to gobble up all that they can eat. Little altars of food with sticks of incense were left out higgledy-piggledy inviting these lost souls to imbibe what us humans had left out for them. In this way, families of humans will be protected from disasters.

Ah Mah made sure that three bowls of rice and a bunch of bananas and three cups of water were left out at the foot of the banyan tree outside our house to appease any starving souls floating by, especially those of Ah Gong and Tua Ko, and perhaps a friend of theirs, she said. Three sticks of incense, one for the Heavenly Kingdom, one for the Earth God, and one for the Guardian of Hell, were stuck into each mound of rice to attract the ghosts.

Ah Mah would also line our threshold with bags of dirt. We had to cross over these bags when entering the house like entering a temple, right leg followed by the left, because we are women, over the make-shift threshold. These bags of dirt formed a raised doorway, preventing hungry ghosts from entering the house looking for more food. Ghosts can only glide on the earth and cannot cross over thresholds because they have no feet.

'We don't want your Ah Gong to come back and bother us with his spirit,' Ah Mah explained as I helped her with the dirt bags. 'Now, go and help your mother seal the back door.'

On my way to the kitchen, cradling a sack of dirt like a baby, I bow habitually before the altar where Ah Gong's spirit tablet sits next to Tua Ko's. Ah Gong died tragically long before I was born. He was a rickshaw puller and an opium addict, and passed away from an overdose one day. Ah Mah howled, Ma told me, because there would now be nobody to bring home any money. Her dedication to the Guanyin goddess increased tenfold after Ah Gong's death. She prays to the goddess every day to protect us from evil.

'Why was my grandfather addicted to opium, Ma?' I asked Mother as I placed the bag of dirt near the kitchen door. Ma was leaning on the door jamb resting, looking out into the backyard. She was almost done lining the threshold of our kitchen door. There was one more dirt bag left to close the gap.

'A rickshaw puller's work is hard work, bitter work,' Ma said turning around to look at me, 'opium eased his aches and made your Ah Gong sleep better.'

'But he died from it, Ma.'

'Unfortunately, yes, what started out as something good, medicine, became something bad, a drug, that lulled him into the hands of Yama, the god of death. His spirit is not a happy one, Mei, so we need to make him happy with these gifts or he will not protect us … but will haunt us instead …'

Ma bent over to drag the bag of dirt towards the gap and placed it at the threshold.

'… we also don't want your Elder Aunty, your Tua Ko, to come back and haunt us either,' Ma continued as she finished up on shutting the ghosts out.

'What happened to Tua Ko, Ma?'

'Well, the death of your father's sister was also a sad one,' Mother sighed, 'Fate can be both benevolent and cruel.'

I never really got to know my Elder Aunt's story, and Ma didn't say much more than this. We didn't talk about these unhappy days much. But we never forget Ah Gong and Tua Ko during the Hungry Ghost Month.

When I was about ten years old in the lunar calendar, during the Feast of the Hungry Ghost, our village home was burnt to the ground. A careless spark caught by an errant breeze lodged itself in one of the coconut fronds covering our roof. Ah Mah was praying by the family altar in the front room when she caught a smokey whiff. Smoke in the air was not uncommon in our kampung, especially during the month when hungry spirits roamed the world greedily imbibing the food and fire offerings made to them, but this whiff was too close to home, and Ah Mah woke Ma up. By then, the roof at the back of our house was scorched amber and burning. Our neighbour Uncle Cheong came with buckets of water to throw at the roof. Ma was doing the same while Ah Mah, Huat and I stood nearby watching helplessly as more and more neighbours came to throw buckets of water at our house. But the fire was strong, and like a hungry ghost, it swallowed our wooden hut up in no time. Ah Mah managed to salvage the statue of Guanyin and Ah Gong's ancestral tablet, along with some of our clothes before these could be consumed by the angry licking flames. And just like this, we were made homeless. Ma wailed so loudly that the neighbours ran home in fear.

Chapter 5

Uncle Cheong was always a good neighbour. He is Mother's distant cousin and knows our family well. We moved in with his family as our house was reduced to embers like the charcoal in the stove when the cooking was done. Uncle Cheong is married to Aunty Eng from Penang. She is sallow-skinned and has dark circles around her eyes, making her look like a panda. Aunty Eng has difficulty sleeping and is a sleepwalker.

They have three children—all girls. Aunty Eng was always trying for a boy. She favoured Huat over me, perhaps it is because Huat is special. He has a gap between his big and second toe, which Aunty Eng said was a sign from the Goddess Mazu and that Ah Huat would bring the family good fortune. Huat means to prosper in Fukien.

While Ah Mah continued to pay obeisance to Goddess Guanyin, who is the patron Goddess of fertility and compassion, Uncle Cheong and Aunty Eng evoked the spirit of Mazu, Goddess of the Sea, and patron saint of sailors and fishermen. Uncle Cheong had come to the Southern Seas, travelling in a

Chinese junk that was tossed about in the foaming South China Sea like vegetables in a hot wok for weeks on end, before he arrived in Nanyang. The first thing he did was to pay respect to the Goddess, who had protected him from rampaging sea pirates and being eaten alive by sea monsters while at sea. His voyage to Nanyang was surprisingly calm and uneventful, unlike some of his compatriots' who had come before and after him.

The benevolent Goddess Mazu had an altar in Uncle Cheong's house. But the Goddess Guanyin didn't have any space on this altar, so Ah Mah had to ask Uncle Cheong to build her a makeshift one so that the bodhisattva Guanyin had a respectable place to stand. Uncle Cheong was none too pleased but he acquiesced to Ah Mah, and she got an altar to place her Goddess on. He did say to Ah Mah that Goddess Guanyin must not overtake the benevolent position of the Goddess Mazu though. Uncle Cheong greeted his Goddess as Thean Hou Ah Mah whenever he prayed to her as if she was his flesh and blood grandmother. I don't know why anyone would want to quarrel over which Goddess was more benevolent. In my thinking, all Goddesses are kind and will bestow anyone praying to them with good things. But I kept these thoughts to myself.

All of us cramped in one small house was not a pleasant way to live. Ah Mah, Ma and Aunty Eng slept in the bedroom, while their daughters, Huat and I slept on the floor on thin mattresses weaved from dried *lalang* grass. During the ant season, I would often wake up from their bites. Uncle Cheong slept in his hammock which was tied between two trees outside their yard. This way, he's not bothered by ants. But the bats hanging from the branches above would sometimes pelt him with their droppings. Behind the yard was the jungle, so thick and luscious that you can't see beyond it. The villagers foraged in the jungle for food sometimes, although they were not allowed to. There was a story of how an elderly villager by the name of Ah Wang who was taken alive by a fierce beast with stripes one day. This beast was like a giant cat, it is said, though I have never seen one. Ah Wang was never found. What remained of him was one rubber shoe and a long trail of blood.

My distant cousins are younger than me and Huat. So, I was charged to look after them instead of going to school. I would've loved to attend some classes but we can't afford the fees. So I don't know how to read or write. But I can read the lines of one's palms, the expressions on one's face, and the tea leaves at the bottom of the cup with such accuracy that people have started to take my word for it, especially my Aunty Eng.

'Tell me what these tea leaves say, Mei,' Aunty Eng would ask me, 'tell me that I would soon have a son.'

I would tell her what I saw in the patterns the tea leaves left behind, and she would listen and nod. I usually kept the unlucky signs to myself. What point was there to frighten an already fearful woman?

Aunty Eng worked in the gentlemen's club up the hill, where important men in suits meet for drinks and a game involving a long stick and some plastic balls that make a pong sound when they collide. Aunty Eng called the game *Beelat* which is how the gentlemen called it, she said. She also said that the balls must remain on the long wooden table lined with a smooth green cloth; it's furry when you run your hands over the cloth, Aunty Eng said. There were pockets at the sides of the table and the aim of the game was to use the long stick to send the balls into the pockets. She learned how the game was played by watching the men through a gap in the toilet door. She was in charge of cleaning the toilets in the club and when there was a game on, her job was to serve the male members a cold towel for freshening up each time they used the rest-room. Those were always good tip days, she told me. When she went to work, I looked after all the children. Ah Mah kept a supervising eye as she couldn't really help me chase the kids about or wash them under the communal pump. Aunty Eng said that at the club, the floors of the toilets were made of a type of white stone that came from far away and she had to scrub them until they shone. And, the place where you do your thing was not a hole in the ground like ours but a type of bowl, that you had to sit on. There was even a cover for when you've finished. She was not allowed to use the bowl, of course. The workers had their own toilet which was a squatting one, like ours in the kampung, except that it was made of ceramic. Water flowed out of taps, she told us, and that nobody had to use any communal pump because of that. I tried to imagine what life would be like for those with toilets like that.

Soon the house got too crowded for all of us.

'Ching, you can't live with us anymore,' Uncle Cheong told Ma just before the next seventh lunar month, 'the house too small. My girls growing and your Ah Mei no need to look after them so much anymore. And, Mei also need to start earning money for the family.'

'Brother, where can I go?' Ma's voice was strained with panic. Worried eyes looked towards Huat and me.

'There's a block of flats near here. Rent is cheaper than most places. You and Mother Ah Mah can take a small flat there. Mei has to start work, so make sure you find her work where you can. Mother Ah Mah can look after Huat.'

Ma packed all that we had in our possession into cloth parcels gratefully. We moved them slowly day by day to the new place with Uncle Cheong's help. As we didn't have too many of these parcels to move, we were in our tiny flat by the second day.

The flat had a small kitchen and not much else. The only two pieces of furniture were an old bed with a soggy mattress and a threadbare sofa. We didn't know for how long the rain had been pouring down on the mattress from a hole above, but Uncle Cheong mended the hole in no time.

'You are a good man, Cheong,' Ma said, 'we can never thank you enough.'

'No, no, it is only right that we help one another, Ching,' he told Ma. 'We are far away from our families and must form new ones in this land.'

For the few days that the mattress dried in the sun, Ah Mah slept on the sofa. As soon as the mattress was all dried up, the musty smell lingering in the flat disappeared. A couple of whacks with a rattan paddle, that we had borrowed from Uncle Cheong, cleared the dust that had lodged in the disused mattress. Ah Mah had a bed. We had taken our grass mats with us, so Huat, Mother and I slept on those.

Ma seemed a little happier in this flat. I think it's because she felt more independent and not so reliant on Uncle Cheong anymore. Ah Mah looked after Ah Huat when Ma and I went to work. Ma had a job washing clothes for a wealthy family in town. The perks of the job were few but at least, she was allowed to have the clothes that the family didn't want or couldn't wear anymore. That was how I ended up with pretty sets of samfoo and blouses. Ma's family had a girl who was kind enough to give me all her old clothes.

Not long after we moved out of Uncle Cheong's house, I started to work washing clothes for another family a few doors down from Ma's work. It wasn't easy at first. I felt bad because I had been taking care of Huat for so long before my new job that I missed him and I was also worried about how Ah Mah would cope on her own. Huat would cry each morning when I left and this tugged at my heart so much.

I would leave for work really early when it was still dark. It took an hour to walk to the house in town and a whole day to wash everyone's clothes. I only needed to do this three times a week, thankfully. The rest of the week, I earned extra money by sewing and mending the family's clothes. They liked my needlework and Madam's friends often complimented her on a new skirt that I had made or a flower that I had embroidered on her blouse. I soon had other little jobs sewing and mending which I loved. Elizabeth Smith, my madam, was kind and she didn't mind if I took time out to help her friends, who were always generous enough to tip me, mend their cloths.

Elizabeth, you must look at how gorgeous these peonies and phoenixes are that Mei has embroidered on my blouse.

Look at these stitches, aren't they exquisite?

Pity that a talented seamstress like her should be washing clothes.

Frankly, I don't know how I got to be so good at sewing. It's not like I had the chance to sew much when I was younger. I just know that when I pick up a needle and pull a thread through its eye, something magical happens. Watching the needle go in and out and seeing those stitches in different colours calm me.

I had Sundays to rest because the family said Sundays are days of rest as God had said in the Bible. I didn't know what this book was but I knew that the Bible was an important book for the Smith family. They had one displayed in a glass case in the living room. I saw it when I took some ironed washing to put away in Madam Elizabeth's room one day.

Working for the Smiths, we were not lacking in clothing. When John, the Smith son, outgrew his shorts and shirts, Madam Elizabeth gave them to me for Huat. Ah Huat is not like the boys his age, he didn't play very much with the few boys in the compound. They mostly left him alone and would occasionally tease him. Ah Huat is a good boy, docile, and he keeps himself to himself. He always saved the brightest smile for me.

This was what made coming home after a long day of scrubbing worthwhile.

* * *

I feed the last of the paper ingots to the fire and stand back to watch it consume the Hell currency. The flames dance and spark, mesmerizing me. I think of Ah Mah who must be burning paper money right now. My thoughts flash to Ma, knowing that she must be missing me, and they remain on Huat before Ah Wan Jie's voice brings me back to the Lee compound.

'I doubt you'll get to sew much here, Mei, because Number One Madam has her own seamstress,' Ah Wan Jie says after I've finished answering all her questions about my family.

Then, she adds, 'As for Huat, you must forget him. You'll never see him again.'

Her eyes clasp on mine when she said this and I see behind them a world—empty, dark, and lonely.

Chapter 6

Cantonment Estate, 1931, the morning before the Hungry Ghost Month

It is the eve of the full moon, a day after my birthday. It's still dark out but the birdsong tells me that it's morning. I lie on my mat, allowing myself to wake up a little more. This morning I feel different. Grown up. I can't believe that I am already sixteen. The Metal Goat year has been a good one so far and the Water Monkey year would be even better. Something is going to change in the new lunar year. I feel it in my bones. Another year after, in the year of the Water Rooster, I could be married, if Ma finds the right boy for me. Eighteen is a right age for marriage, Ma always said.

'Rabbit girls, like you, make good wives. You're devoted, considerate and generous,' Ma said yesterday after she wished me happy birthday and giving me a hard-boiled egg that she had stained red. 'I'm sure we'll find you a good match when the time comes.'

By the time Ma was around my age, she had sailed, alone, across the China Sea to Malaya to marry my father. She was seventeen. By eighteen, she was already a mother. To a stillborn boy. I came not long after and between my birth and Huat's, there were some more, all dying before they were fully grown. There seemed to be an imbalance of yin and yang in Ma's blood flow. Herbal medicines would perhaps remedy this, but we don't have enough money for medication.

I'm small for my age. I could pass for being twelve, maybe thirteen. But physically, I'm no longer a girl. I started my monthly bleeds a year ago and Ma said that I must guard my treasure house as best as I can.

'Don't let any boy or man steal your jewel, your bride price,' she said when my first bleed started.

I have noticed that the men in the compound are starting to look at me with a curious glow in their eyes. Ma has noticed too. Where I was once flat as pancakes, there are now buds sprouting and I need a new piece of clothing to hide my growing breasts. Just a month before I turned sixteen, Ma asked her lady boss if she could have some of the young mistress's brasseries, and because the lady of the house was kind, she handed Ma two of them for me.

I am to wear these short tunics with an elastic band under my thin samfoo top to cover my breasts, Ma tells me. I learned how to put this short tunic on by fiddling with one. It wasn't that hard. Now, I waste no time at all putting a brassiere on. Because the cotton is of quality, it doesn't scratch me. It stretches over my growing chest adding a protective layer, hiding my budding nipples from untoward attention. I am so glad for them.

'But no piece of clothing would really protect a woman from the prowling monster that is a man's desire,' Ma cautioned me, 'so always be careful. Your bride price belongs to your husband.'

Since Ah Pa's departure to work in the city, Ma's spirit has improved. She is cooking properly again. A few days ago, she bought an old wok from the ironmonger in town that she lugged home on her back by looping a rope on each wok handle and wearing the wok on her shoulders.

'Look, come and look, what I've got,' Ma gestured to us cheerfully.

We stood around her as she untied the black wok and put it down on the floor. It was big enough for Huat to have a bath in and not light either.

'This was what the restaurant in town threw out,' Ma told us, 'I asked the ironmonger and he sold it to me for a good price. I'll pay him weekly until the debt is paid up.'

Ma had loved cooking when we lived in the kampung. That was when Ah Pa sent money home. She used to fry the vegetables in an old clay pot, which is now broken. She always saved the oil for another time. She stored the used oil in an old rice bowl that had a chipped rim. With the new wok, the shine in her eyes returned. I loved the vegetable fritters that she used to cook in the old clay pot, but with the new wok, the fritters taste even better. Ma always made magic in the kitchen by inventing new dishes with whatever little ingredients we had.

'Pity I can't work in the restaurants as a cook,' she said one evening while slicing a square of tofu, 'I'd make more money there than washing clothes.'

I wondered why it is only men who are allowed to work in the kitchens at restaurants when they don't cook at home like the womenfolk. Ah Pa can't cook, so perhaps that was the reason he became a baker instead.

'Ma,' I said, 'you could get a job as a cook in a rich man's house.'

'Silly goose, who would employ me?' She replied, caressing me on my head. 'These rich folks eat differently from us.

They may be Chinese but they like their sambals, which I don't know how to make. And their curries, so many different types too, and all so spicy.'

'But you can learn.'

'Of course, but first I need to get a job there, and who is going to employ me when they see my hands, bleeding like this?'

I watched Ma grimace as she chopped up some garlic and ginger before tossing them into her new wok. Hours of scrubbing, rinsing and wringing laundry have put cuts and blisters on her hands.

A sizzle and a stir and the flat permeated with the aromas of my childhood.

* * *

I find Ma in the kitchen preparing our breakfast. She works in the dimness, saving on candles. She is washing rice to make our morning congee. There's a dish of pickled mustard leaves to go with the congee ready on the small dining table. I pick up the buckets that I need to fetch fresh water. It usually takes me three or four trips back and forth to fill up our water jar in the kitchen. Ma had found a disused Shanghai jar by the road one night. A piece is missing at the mouth, but the jar still holds water. She rolled it back and with a neighbour's help was able to bring it up to the flat.

'Going to the pump, but will do the prayers first.'

'You're a good girl, Mei,' Ma says. 'What would I do without you?'

I love this time of the day. It's a new day and I am thankful that I have my family around me when I wake up.

Chapter 7

I have just finished with the prayers and am getting ready to fetch water from the pump when a boy in a uniform arrives at our doorstep. He has a satchel across his shoulder and is wearing a cap that makes him look like a policeman. He stands at our open front door holding a piece of paper.

'A message for you,' he says, while rubbing sleep from his eyes.

Ah Mah stops folding ingots and Ma heads to the front door. 'What is it?' she asks the messenger boy.

As none of us can read, he reads the message out for us.

I am to pack my bags and leave with him for the city. I am too shocked to say anything. Ma is confused and wants to know who has sent the boy.

'Eminent Mister Lee,' he replies, irritation visible in his voice.

'But how I can send my girl away, just like that?' Ma asks, exasperation loud in hers.

'Eminent Mister Lee said that he had paid a lot of good money for Ah Mei,' he answers, sounding a little high-strung now.

'Money? What money? I've not seen any of this money that your Eminent Mister Lee has spent on my Ah Mei.'

'Did Ah Leong sell her hand in marriage to the Lee house?' Ah Mah asks gruffly amidst the back and forth of the confusing conversation that she has been listening in to.

'Mother, how could Ah Leong do this? Your son would never sell our daughter.' Her voice is coloured with desperation and tinged with helplessness.

'Hnh,' Ah Mah sneers, 'a gambler would do anything for the next bet.'

I have never heard Ah Mah speak so disparagingly about Ah Pa before. After all, he is her only living child since Tua Ko's death, and a son too. I am a ball of confusion.

I listen to Ma exchanging more words with the messenger boy, who doesn't look all that much older than me on closer inspection. But she has no power nor might to stop the messenger boy from taking me away. He reads the last sentence in the letter, 'Do not resist or Ah Leong will suffer.'

'Didn't I say, didn't I say,' Ah Mah's screeches as soon as the messenger boy finishes reading.

'What have I done to deserve this, Guanyin Goddess,' Ah Mah laments loudly, while she knelt in front of the Goddess's altar. 'Have pity on me. First an opium addict of a husband, then a daughter who drowned, and now a son who is willing to sell his own flesh and blood.'

Ah Mah's wails mix with moans as she bows her head on the ground. I watch her prostrated in a position of humility and deference and my heart fills with sorrow and shame.

Ma tells me to pack a few pieces of clothing in a cloth bag. She gives me her only pair of good shoes, she will have to wear slippers made from car tyres for the time being, she says.

Ah Huat wakes up from all the commotion and saunters up to me from his corner of the room. His cheeks are streaked with dirt and tears. He grabs me around the waist, unwilling to let go. His dribble soaks into my top and I have to pull him away.

'Don't go, Mei-jie, don't go!'

There is something about Ah Huat that tugs at my heart strings. I don't know what it is. I was eight years old when he was born. Ah Pa was growing agitated that I was the only child for so long and a girl at that.

'Useless girl,' he would say to Ma, 'another mouth to feed. What can she do for me and the family?'

Then when Huat was finally born, Ah Pa had wanted to leave him in the city to families desperate for sons.

'They're the ones who can afford a boy like him,' Ah Pa shouted banging his hands on the dining table, 'they can pick him up by the rubbish bin.'

I didn't understand what he meant because all sons are precious. How could Ah Pa just toss him away like an unwanted girl? If it were not for Uncle Cheong, Ah Huat would not be alive today. Huat means to prosper in my language. So he is a lucky boy.

After Uncle Cheong's intervention, the scoldings started, the beatings and the blaming followed soon after.

'Useless girl, useless boy, useless woman,' he spat the words at Ma.

'Ah Fook,' Ma replied, holding me close, 'don't judge our Ah Mei. She was born with a lucky knot stuck to her back.'

Perhaps Ma was referring to the mole that sits right smack on my spinal cord just at the base of my skull. If I run my fingers through my hair, I can feel the lump. I was rubbing my mole when heat spread across my right cheek at the contact of Ah Pa's hand. I shrank into my mother's embrace, my eyes stinging with tears.

'Such bad luck to be surrounded by all of you—good for nothing, make me lose money all the time,' he screamed at me and Ma, and then mauled his way out of the house. I gulped down my relief as Ah Pa tore past Ah Huat sleeping in an old drawer without hurting him.

That was the last time anyone of us saw him again.

* * *

'Take this amulet and wear it every day,' Ah Mah says quietly to me as I pack up the last of my things, 'pin it to the inside of your blouse.'

Ah Mah hands me a triangular glass pendant attached to a pin encasing a folded piece of yellow paper filled with red inscriptions. It is the size of my thumb, not heavy. The inscriptions are prayers that the Abbot in the Taoist temple had written out for her some years ago. A protection against evil.

It is Ma's turn to cry. The delay must have been the time she needed to process the reality of the situation. Her shoulders heave up and down as muffled sounds of weeping escape from her lips. She is rummaging through a rusty biscuit tin. I stand there glued to the spot, as I don't know what to do or say to comfort her. I don't want to go but what choice do I have?

'Wait, Mei,' Ma speaks in between sobs, 'take this.'

She presses a small bag made of red cloth into my palms. She closes my hand into a fist and wraps hers around it. She squeezes my hand three times and mouths I love you.

'This is all I have. It was the only precious thing that my mother gave me before I boarded the ship that took me here to marry your father. I have kept it safely away all these years for you. For a special day. This day is special in its own way, wear the necklace always.'

I can hardly see her through my blur of tears. But her voice is clear like the first birdsong in the morning. *Wear the necklace always.*

'Oy, what is taking you so long?' the messenger boy grumbles, shuffling back and forth.

My family stands by the door as I follow the messenger boy, who has cycled to our shanty village, down the corridor and out of the compound. He wheels his vehicle as I walk alongside. I turn around and look at my home and my family for the last time. I sniff the air to bottle it in a jar I keep in my mind. I look towards the red door, and see Ma, Ah Mah and Huat getting smaller and smaller the further away I go. Something tells me that I will never see this flat and my family again.

Chapter 8

'Do you know why you're being sent to Eminent Mister Lee's house?' He asks me as soon as we are out of the compound.

'What?' I reply, irritated.

My face is wet from tears, my nose dribbling. Huat's wailing is still thrumming in my ears and the heart-rending vision of Ma weeping uncontrollably clings to the edges of my memory refusing to let go. *What will they do now? Who will look after Huat? When will I be coming home again?*

'Do you know why you're leaving?' He probes again.

'No, do you?' I am suddenly hopeful. Maybe he has an answer.

'Oh, I don't know, I thought you knew.'

I could only hazard a guess. I am to be married to somebody in the Lee family? Who *is* the Eminent Mister Lee?

'Am I going to be married, you know?' At this thought, I wipe my face and nose with the end of my blouse.

The messenger boy shrugs his shoulders and begins whistling a song. I walk silently beside him, wondering where the stretch of road ahead will take me.

It is getting lighter. I love this time in the morning when the air is humid but cool, and a blanket of dew hangs above the lalang grass waiting to descend. It will disappear when the sun comes out and depending on what kind of sun it is, I can always tell if the day will be scorching or overcast. During the monsoon season, the smell of rain lingers in the air and I would prepare for it by putting out our buckets to collect the rain fall. At home, Ma would already be up and cooking our breakfast. It's usually some gruel of rice porridge which we ate with pickled mustard greens, and if we had extra money, some fried anchovies. Ah Mah would salt fresh mustard leaves and then soak them in a brine solution before stuffing them away in a ceramic jar to preserve. This way they keep for months. She would do the same with duck eggs that, if we're lucky, we found around the kampung. After moving to our flat, we had to do away with salted duck eggs. Apart from several smaller jobs in the kampung, my main jobs were to go fetch water from the pump and light three joss sticks for Guanyin Goddess, Ah Gong and Tua Ko. The roosters calling and the chirping of the insects fading away, coming back again when night fell, were signs of life that I held on to tightly. These signs are more important now because I may never see them again. I feel desperate just thinking about this. I bite back the bitter tears welling up again. To distract myself, I turn my attention to other things.

'Boy-ah, how long more to Eminent Mister Lee's house? What is your name, anyway?'

'I am Ban Guan. We are heading to the city, it's still a long way off. I had to cycle to your house in the middle of the night. Don't know why so urgent.'

'So urgent?'

'Yeah, usually, I deliver a message and a rickshaw comes to pick the girl up.'

'What is a rickshaw?'

'Aiya, you don't know? It's like chair with wheels pulled by a man. You sit on chair and the man pulls you along until you reach where you want to go.'

I marvel at Ban Guan's words and try to imagine what a chair with wheels being pulled by a man looks like. A shudder of excitement runs through me. I don't know if I should be this excited since my fate is pretty much uncertain at this point.

'You can read. How?'

'Oh, it's nothing. My father was the village school master until he died. I can't read all that well, lah. But the notes always say the same things.'

There is no emotion in his voice. If Ah Pa died, I would feel some sadness, although I don't really know him at all. He had left that long ago I don't remember him much anymore.

'Sorry to hear about his death. May the Goddess bless his soul.'

'Thank you. It's nothing, lah. He died of sickness. Blood in his lungs, the doctor said.'

Blood in his lungs. What kind of ghost would he be?

The sun is almost overhead now. We must have walked miles because my feet are beginning to feel very sore and the jungle is now behind us. We have also passed the cemetery, where Ah Gong is buried in the pauper's section. This tells me that we are now quite a long way from the flat. The last time I saw Ah Gong was last year during the Qing Ming Festival. Ma, Ah Mah, Huat and I went to sweep his grave and bring him some food and new clothes, which we set on fire so that the fumes will bring his desires to the Heavenly Kingdom. Ah Mah had said that Ah Gong told her he wanted new clothes in a dream. I remember now how much we had to walk lugging food and sacrificial items just to get to his grave before the sun became too strong.

Ban Guan wants to stop and have something to eat. There is a stall selling fried *mee hoon* by the side of the street. I love this rice noodles too, but I don't have any money to buy food. Instead of giving me money, Ma had pressed something into my hands, something hard wrapped in a red satin cloth. *Take this and wear it always. I have nothing to give you except this precious thing that my mother had left to me before I crossed the seas* … was all she had said.

I sit on a stone under a flame of the forest tree while Ban Guan orders his food. The smell of fried garlic and rice noodles with egg makes me salivate. I am hungry too. As he eats, I unwrap Mother's gift. A jade Guanyin gleams at me from its silky red blanket. She is strung on a yellow chain so golden that it glitters in the noon sun. I put the Goddess around my neck and it comes down, resting nicely between my collar bones. As I tighten the clasp, I feel heat emanating from the pendant. I rub it and the heat transfers to my fingers. Strange. But I think nothing much of it because my stomach takes up all of my attention.

'Here, have some before we leave, a long way more.'

Ban Guan hasn't forgotten me after all. I finish up the last of his fried mee hoon, wipe my mouth with the back of my right hand, and get up to leave.

'Aye, I know why so urgent,' Ban Guan says excitedly.

'Why?'

'It's the Hungry Ghost Month tomorrow, and if they don't come and get you now, Eminent Mister Lee's family will have to wait another month for a new mui tsai.'

He beams at me, proud that he had come up with an answer. Ban Guan is right. Nobody travels during this inauspicious month.

Mui tsai?

Chapter 9

Singapore town, May 1932

The man with the cloudy eye is looking at me. I hold his gaze. We are separated by the Lee household's main gate; the gate that opens out to the main road, which is used only by Ah Chin when he drives the Eminent Mister Lee out. The gate is made of ornate steel with a winding five-claw dragon on one side and a flaming phoenix on the other. Ah Yoke doesn't see the man. She never does. I continue to hold the man's glassy gaze for half a minute more, then look away. He can't do anything, standing there beyond the Lee compound by the banyan tree. I am protected by my amulet from Ah Mah. I am also protected by the Goddess. But I am concerned that Ah Yoke isn't. I stroke my Guanyin pendant for extra protection, rubbing her between my right thumb and index finger, invoking her power. I can feel the lines carved into the jade that the artist had incised to make the Goddess. I feel the heat of Guanyin Mother's energy.

I put my right arm around Ah Yoke and guide her to turn left at the *pintu pagar*. This special wooden swinging door at the front of the house, Ah Wan Jie told me, is found in all houses owned by the Peranakan-Chinese and is always intricately carved; the Lee's one is made of teak and painted in gold. As the pintu pagar is not a full-sized door, its job when shut is to allow the main door of the house to stay open, letting in light and air into the *tia besar*, the front room, while protecting the inhabitants, especially the female members, of the house from prying eyes. To the left of the pintu pagar, at the end of a corridor the length of the house, is a side wall. The Lee house shares a wall with its neighbour on the right but there's no other house on its left. The thick wall on its left is an outer side wall. There is an iron side gate there and we step out of the house through this gate. The gate opens out to a side street where rickshaw pullers usually park to rest. This is the side street that Hassan takes to get to the alleyway at the back of the house. Holding Ah Yoke's hand tightly in mine, I say a prayer asking Guanyin Mother to pass her protective energy from me to Ah Yoke. I close the gate and it shuts with a loud clang. I see a vacant rickshaw and gesture to the puller.

'Lau Pa Sat, uncle.' Ah Yoke and I climb on to our rickshaw. The seat is good only for one, so I take my position, sitting with my knees to my chin by Ah Yoke's feet, on the foot rest. The rickshaw puller makes sure that Ah Yoke is shaded before he returns to the front of his vehicle. He adjusts his straw hat, dabs his sweaty brows with a face towel that hangs around his neck, bends down and lifts the bars attached to the seat, and I feel myself sliding backwards. With a slight jerk he starts to jog, barefoot. We are off, slowly at first and speeding up when the puller has gained momentum. It wasn't so long ago that I didn't know what a rickshaw was. *A chair with wheels*, Ban Guan had said. It's incredible how my life has changed since living with the Lees.

The rickshaw puller stops us some distance away from the morning market. I wanted him to so that I can peek inside Encik Abdullah's to see what Hassan is doing. I wait for some motor cars to pass by first and holding Ah Yoke's hand tightly, we cross the street and walk briskly towards the market, heading closer to Abdullah's Sundries Shop. I can sense that it will be another hot and humid day; the air is clammy and still. It hasn't been raining lately and the land is arid and dusty. I watch a cloud of dust circle around our feet. I am grateful for covered feet. I am wearing the canvas shoes that Ah Wan Jie had given me.

Hassan is at the front of the shop, the open entrance providing me with a full view. He is fanning Encik Abdullah with a hand-held foldable fan instead of stacking shelves. Sometimes, when the weather is really hot, Hassan uses another type of fan. We have quite a few of those at the Lee house. I find it hard to say my house, although it is my house since I now live there. The fans at the Lee's house can't be folded up and is made of dried grass crisscrossed to form the body of the fan. For guests, Number One Madam, would ask the servants to bring out silk fans with beautiful embroidered peonies and phoenixes on the body. The handles are made with special silk threads plaited until they formed a thick and hard loop.

'Harder, boy, fan harder, it's so hot,' Encik Abdullah commands Hassan, his voice travelling towards me. The heat must be making him irritable.

Hassan speeds up, waving the fan up and down briskly at Encik Abdullah who I see seated behind his counter in a white man's singlet. Sweat is running down the sides of Hassan's face. And as he fans Encik Abdullah with one hand, he is mopping his face with the sleeve of his shirt, shrugging his left shoulder as he does this. My heart stirs and squeezes in sympathy.

Hassan catches my eye as Ah Yoke and I walk past the shop. He smiles at me, his eyes dancing with excitement and I nod back at him, cautious that nobody sees us communicating this way. I have learnt to be surreptitious in my movements. I could be nodding to Encik Abdullah, which is the impression I want to give, and Encik Abdullah nods back at me.

'Cook want something today?' Encik Abdullah shouts out in Malay. 'I have some fresh curry powder for curries, freshly ground, just for her.' He finishes in Hokkien.

'No, *terima kasih*, Pak Abdullah. Not this morning. She wants some *buah keluak*, pork and coriander today.' I have started to greet Encik Abdullah with the honorific 'Pak', sounding just like Hassan.

'Ah, making that haram dish again,' he replies in disgust. 'I don't know how the Peranakans can speak Malay but eat pork. Ok, come to me when she needs some good chilli powder and curries, don't forget,' he sends me off with a cheerful note. I continue walking towards the open-air market.

The first day I spoke to Hassan was little over a month after I had started work looking after Ah Yoke. Ah Wan Jie had sent me out to Encik Abdullah's Sundries Shop for a bag of oil, barley pearls, and a packet of rock sugar.

'Number One Madam wants some barley water made. She's feeling heaty. Mei, I'm in pain, can you go and get the ingredients at Encik Abdullah's. Get extra, so we can have some too. Good for taking the heat away … and whilst you're there, better get some onions, garlic and rice … and don't forget, bargain … '

The temperatures were high during the day as is the usual for September, but the night breezes blowing in from the Java Sea did bring some respite at least. Some barley water would be good for everyone. Due to the weather, Ah Wan Jie's arthritis was playing up and her hands and knees were bloated with pain.

Her moans and groans filled the kitchen with anguish. She had asked Number One Madam's rickshaw puller to take me to Encik Abdullah's since the madam and her lady friends were busy playing mahjong. Encik Abdullah was not in the shop that day, so it was Hassan who served me.

'Miss, what can I get you?' his voice was low and he had a twinkle in his eye when he spoke. 'Today, Abdullah's Sundries has a special offer. Oil for twenty cents, curries for five cents.'

There was a playfulness in his voice that made me giggle. I wished I hadn't but I couldn't help myself.

'Ah, the young Miss finds me funny, does she?'

'Barley and rock sugar,' I said in a serious tone, 'and add some garlic and onions too, no charge. Please deliver them to the Lee house at Neil Road.'

I surprised myself for ordering extras for free. I don't know where I had found a voice to do that. As Hassan picked the goods I'd ordered, I noticed how dextrous he was and how his fingers were quick and nimble, dropping bulbs and tubers into a paper bag. I saw how generous he was too with my order, slipping in more than I'd asked for.

My skin is pale next to his, but like me, he has black hair. His was shiny and thick that day like he had slicked it with oil. His arms and legs are long, sinewy, and although he was a burst of energy, he was light on his feet. When he smiled, a straight line of teeth like a row of white tiles flashed at me.

'Don't be so fierce, my lady, star of the sky,' Hassan teased, 'I will do your bidding if you give me a smile. I'm sure your sweet smile will stir the embers of my loving heart. Your smile would be brighter than all the nine suns in the sky. You, my lady, are the moon that will outshine any sun.'

Hassan's words amused me. But something behind him fizzled out the good humour.

Behind Hassan was the figure of Encik Abdullah inching closer and closer until he delivered a whack to Hassan's head, making him yelp in surprise. My heart flinched.

'What are you doing, you idiot?' thundered Encik Abdullah, 'finish up the order and stop your flirting. Are you out of your head?'

Hassan scurried away to pack up my orders as I paid Encik Abdullah.

'Don't be caught by his sweet words,' Encik Abdullah cautioned in a tone tinged with compassion. 'At seventeen, he fancies himself a poet, always reading Tagore and composing poetry. Don't indulge him. Where to send the goods, young Miss?'

'Neil Road, Encik,' I replied, 'for the Lee house.'

'Ah—then you must be the new mui ... the ... the new servant girl.' Encik Abdullah said with some hesitance. 'What's your name?' His dark brown eyes peeked out at me from under thick bushy eyebrows. He held my gaze for few seconds before I answered him.

'Ah Mei.'

He nodded and added, '... remember, don't indulge him ... Hassan ... I mean, don't indulge his poetry, Mei.' There was now an urgency in his voice.

I was caught between being curious about what this thing called poetry was and heeding Encik Abdullah's cautionary words. Who is Tagore? And me indulge Hassan? I would never do such a thing. A proper girl never indulges a boy. Yet, my heart raced. I couldn't wait to hear Hassan's voice again.

Chapter 10

The market is heaving. Domestic helpers and elderly women are haggling with store owners at the vegetable section over the prices of light purple brinjals, fiery red chillies, and telescopes of green bitter gourds and cucumbers. A chicken squawks as its head is yanked off, freshly slaughtered for a waiting customer. The defeathering process will begin soon after the half-dead bird is doused in a vat of boiling water. Cleavers hack chunks of pork or goat into smaller pieces while other butchers sharpen their knives against a metal rod, the screeching scratch of blade against metal grating me. A mélange of languages and the woody, earthy scents of herbs and spices find their way into my ear and up my nose. We are in a melting pot of lively chatter churning with sounds of Tamil, Malay, Kristang, Cantonese and Fukienese all being stirred together with the smells of turmeric, ginger, garlic, fresh coriander and spicy chillies.

I speak Cantonese myself because that was what Ma spoke to me in, but I have learnt some of the course sounding words of the Fukienese dialect, Ah Pa's language, from listening in on the conversations at the Lee household and by asking Ah Wan Jie to teach me some words. Although the Lee family is Fukienese, they speak mostly Malay amongst themselves, except for Number One Madam who prefers Fukien. Being surrounded by Malay means that I have also picked up a few native words here and there.

The buzz is distracting and I mustn't forget what I have come to buy—a piece of pork belly and a bag of buah keluak, the poisonous nut that Number One Madam likes with her pork stew. Ah Wan Jie wants a bunch of coriander too.

I keep Ah Yoke close to me as we jostle with the early morning shoppers. Some people stop to stare at the Lee daughter, whispering behind our backs as we pass. Ah Yoke has an unusually oval face with eyes that resemble crescent moons. She is very fair and is a little on the heavy side. She is older than me, I've been told, but she behaves like a child. What makes people stare is her habit of letting her tongue hang out, the dribble running down her chin, and a cut on her upper lip that splits it in two. Even I find it hard to look at Ah Yoke myself. The hole that is her mouth is like an opening to a cave.

'Close your mouth,' I remind her. Ah Yoke smiles and nods, picking up her bib to wipe a dribble. I nod back at her in approval because these words have become our secret code for her to wipe her mouth. Ah Yoke was born with an overabundance of saliva.

I've never seen someone who loves her food as much as Ah Yoke, and Ah Wan Jie who seems very fond of the Lee daughter always indulges her. No wonder Ah Yoke is slightly rounded in the waist, arms and thighs. She can dress herself and can speak, although, she would rather keep quiet. She reminds me in so many ways of Huat. And like Huat, Ah Yoke has a gap between her big and second toe. A sign of good luck—she is someone who will bring great fortune to her family. Although Number One Madam doesn't talk or see Ah Yoke much, I'm sure that as her mother, she must feel blessed to have such a lucky charm in the family. I must address Ah Yoke as Elder Daughter in Fukienese when I am speaking about her with Number One Madam, Ah Wan Jie has instructed me.

Ah Wan Jie has been with the Lee house for as long as she can remember. She took over from her mother when she passed away, having served generations of the Lee family.

'Be careful, Mei, that you keep a close eye on Ah Yoke,' Ah Wan Jie said to me on the day I arrived. 'Ah Yoke is a special girl.'

I didn't dare ask too much, like why Ah Yoke is special, due to the tone of Ah Wan Jie's voice. But I don't let Ah Yoke out of my sight.

I get the meat, the keluak nut and coriander that Ah Wan Jie had asked for and wave a rickshaw down to take us home. As I settle by Ah Yoke's feet once more, I see the man with the funny eye again. This time he is standing opposite us half hidden by two rickshaw pullers having a rest under a Tembusu tree. I thought I'd lost him in the crowd but there he is staring at me, boring into me with his cloudy eyes. I look away as soon as the rickshaw starts to pull away.

The mole at the top of my spine starts to tingle.

Chapter 11

Lee Kitchen, end of December 1931

'Ah Mei, go and buy me some curry powder, will you?'

I am in the middle of sewing some peonies on a hanky for Ah Yoke when Ah Wan Jie hollers for my help.

'Ah Wan Jie wants you, Mei-jie,' Ah Yoke alerts me looking up from her drawing. It is a beautiful stylised charcoal image of a peony still waiting for her final touches.

'Coming.'

'I would like some curry powder, onions and garlic, and a bag of Jasmine rice,' Ah Wan Jie lists out her items, 'don't forget to tell Encik Abdullah that it's the Thai rice I want. Number One Madam prefers that. And, ask him to deliver the goods immediately. I have a pot of rendang curry to make.'

I love running errands for Ah Wan Jie. My stomach knots in excitement as I help Ah Yoke put away her things and prepare for our outing. It is drizzling lightly, just the usual kind for the last month of the year. I have been taking care of Ah Yoke now for several months, but I still do not know what Number

One Madam and Eminent Mister Lee look like. It's not that I need to meet them but I would like to know what Number One Madam is like at least and how the Eminent Mister Lee is as well. He had just celebrated an important birthday. The house fluttered with commotion but I wasn't part of it. Ah Wan Jie had said that I was to remain invisible, stay in the kitchen. Those were instructions from Number One Madam, Ah Wan Jie had said. Apart from Number One Madam and the Eminent Mister Lee, I know there is a young son, some years older than me, and everyone calls him Master Lee. He's away from the house for most of the time.

I hail a rickshaw to take us to Encik Abdullah's Sundries Shop. Hassan is only a few minutes away.

I love how the shop is filled with the earthy fragrance of all the curry pastes that Encik Abdullah sells. There are wet curries and dry powdered versions and he always advises on what curry mix is suitable for the type of dishes you're cooking. A couple of mui tsai are there doing their errands too. And, Hassan is serving them. I notice that he doesn't behave the same way as he does with me. I am so relieved to know this. I observe him as he picks out the items that one mui tsai is listing. He is meticulous but he doesn't tease her like he teases me. I wait for Hassan to serve me, hoping that he will, as I think back to the first day I met him. That day was a day like today. The shop was buzzing and Hassan was busy bagging onions, garlic, ginger and spices as he is doing now. My heart sinks as Encik Abdullah saunters in my direction.

'Pak, pak, need your help here,' Hassan chirps when he sees me and Encik Abdullah goes to his aid instead.

My heart skips a beat as he nods my way giving me a quick knowing glance.

'*Apa*? What do you want?' Encik Abdullah asks Hassan in an irritated tone.

'Ah Ling Miss here would like some wet curry and only you make the best!'

A disgruntled Encik Abdullah attends to the mui tsai, Ah Ling, from the Chan house, and Hassan glides over to me grinning from ear to ear.

'My moon and star,' he says, 'I have waited a life time for you. Welcome, welcome again to my magic cave.'

My face turns red and I feel the heat rising to my cheeks. Hassan swipes the air as he greets me and his hands brushes against mine. He apologizes profusely in whispers and reassures me that he's not taking advantage.

'You are the star of my night sky, Ah Mei Miss. I will always remain faithful to you.' I see the tips of his brown ears turn a blush pink.

'Some curry powder, onions and garlic, and a bag of Jasmine rice,' I rattle off Ah Wan Jie's list from memory. My lips curl slightly giving Hassan an encouraging half-smile.

'At your service, my Moon Goddess,' he teases again, 'how would you like your curry?'

I hesitate because Ah Wan Jie didn't mention if she wanted the curry mix as a paste or powder. I kicked myself mentally because if I get the wrong one, she would throw a fit.

'For rendang,' I say, hoping this would help.

'Ah, then, you will need a magic potion of the best wet curry paste that Abdullah's Sundries can conjure up.'

'Hassan!' Encik Abdullah hollers from the back. I take a step back from Hassan as I see Ah Ling scurry past stifling a giggle.

'Pak Abdullah, I am serving an important customer. Be with you in a second.'

'He wants me to give him the honorific pak, meaning sir,' Hassan tells me sotto voce. His eyes roll and I sense how Hassan resents being treated this way by his blood uncle. Hassan holds my gaze and I gulp an acknowledgement.

'Hurry up, Hassan, there are deliveries.'

'Coming!' he hollers back to his uncle and then to me he says quietly, 'Mei, I'm serious!'

I nod. Hassan lowers his eyes after giving me a slight smile. I am serious too. But I had no eloquent words to use.

'Meet me at the back of the house when I deliver the goods.'

Despite my hesitation, I find myself nodding my head.

The heat is scorching when we step out of Encik Abdullah's Sundries. It was cooler in there with the thin cotton curtains half drawn. I turn slightly to peek in and see that Hassan is now fanning Encik Abdullah while the older man writes into his ledger.

'He like you,' Ah Yoke giggles, 'he say nice things to you.'

'Shh, Ah Yoke, you mustn't repeat those things, ok?' I sometimes forget that Ah Yoke is attached to me like a shadow. She often doesn't say much, content to observe the scene than add to the cacophony.

'Why he like you?'

I realize that perhaps Ah Yoke doesn't get the urgency of why she must keep mum.

'He likes everyone, Ah Yoke. We are his customers. I'm no different to Ah Ling, the other mui tsai. See?'

Ah Yoke nods, somewhat convinced with my explanation.

'He like you more,' but she says with emphasis.

'It's not true. Let's leave it for now. Just remember that this is our secret and you mustn't repeat anything you've heard to anyone, not even Ah Wan Jie … especially Ah Wan Jie, ok?'

As we climb into our rickshaw, I am suddenly overwhelmed with anxiety. How much does Ah Yoke sense Hassan's feelings for me? More importantly, how much does she sense my feelings for him? I must find a way to keep her sweet. Nobody must know that I even speak to a Muslim boy. I would bring shame to the Lee family and I can't afford to do that. And, nobody must know that I even like Hassan. I mean, I have never seen anyone like me married to anyone like him. It is just not done.

Chapter 12

Ah Wan Jie is in a fix when we arrive home. She is muddle-headed today, undecided about what dishes to prepare.

'What took you so long? Where are the ingredients? I am late in preparation. I will make a pot of chicken curry … beef rendang … some sambal prawns … goodness … I'm all a muddle, Mei—'

'Hassan will be delivering them, Ah Wan Jie. There were too many things to take back with me.'

'Aiya, useless girl, you couldn't even bring back the onions? At least I could start with the *rempah* before the rest of the ingredients come.' She sits down heavily on her stool, grumbling about the dishes for tonight's dinner and Number One Madam's Saturday cherki session. It's her turn to host the gambling session this morning. I notice that Ah Wan Jie's ankles are swollen and she seems distracted.

'Aiyo so many things to do … must cook the dinner dishes first before I leave for the afternoon,' Ah Wan Jie mumbles, 'Ah Mei, help me with the chopping, will you?'

Ah Yoke is about to say something when I shush her.

'Go to my room now and finish up your drawing, Ah Yoke. I will come in a minute.'

She runs off and I help Ah Wan Jie clean some lemon grass stalks, then peel and slice a thumb of ginger. My heart is thumping because I know any minute now, Hassan will be ringing the service bell. What excuse can I give to Ah Wan Jie so I can meet him out in the alley?

'Ah Wan Jie, the chamber pot is almost full in our room. I'll just take them out to be emptied before they overspill.'

Ah Wan Jie harrumphs at me, now too focused on stirring the *chap chye* than pay me more attention. *Cannot overcook the cabbage, must be crunchy*, she mutters on about how important it is to cook this vegetable stew just right according to Eminent Mister Lee's preference. I run to the room, slide the chamber pot slowly from under the bed so I don't spill anything, gag and hold my breath before picking it up.

'Stay here, Ah Yoke. I'll be back soon,' I instruct her and hold my breath again, carrying the chamber pot towards the service door.

Just as I am done emptying the pot into the night soil bucket, Hassan arrives in his bullock cart with all our groceries. I leave the empty chamber pot by the back door before wiping my hands on my pants, neatening my hair and straightening my samfoo top. Then I walk towards the cart with my heart in my throat. He smiles at me, somewhat shyly. The alleyway is empty, except for a few stray cats. Hassan and I have never been this close and together so privately before. He takes my hand and I don't stop him. Waves of sensations I cannot describe stir within me. My womb tugs at the softness of his caress. We linger for a moment in this mild ecstasy. And then, Hassan strokes my right cheek with the back of his fingers and edges his face closer, his lips brushing against mine.

Conscious that we mustn't be doing this, I pull away.

'Sorry Mei, I … I—'

He backs off too and immediately unloads our orders from the cart. One of the buffaloes moves a little, tugging the cart forward before Hassan can stop him. The bag of rice sitting at the edge falls with a thud, spilling pearly grains everywhere. Hassan says words that I don't know could come from his mouth. He starts to sweep the rice back into the hessian sack and I help him, worried that Ah Wan Jie would be furious. Our hands brush each other's as we collaborate to clean up the mess. Even in this state of angst, I feel an electric current sweep up my arms.

'I've got to go, Hassan,' I say as soon as the rice grains have been collected.

'Mei, I really like you. I can't explain these emotions that well up inside me when I think of you.'

I nibble my lower lip in anticipation. I nod to acknowledge his words. *I like you too, Hassan.* I wanted to say but that would be wrong. A girl must not be so demonstrative.

'Let's try to meet out here again. Two days from now.'

I run into the house in panic and elation without responding to Hassan. *What is Hassan saying? What is he asking me to do?* But I am eager to meet him two days from now.

'Hassan, Hassan, you so late, *apa ini*, what's this?' Ah Wan Jie shouts from the stove as Hassan enters with our bag of rice and the rest of the groceries.

I check on Ah Yoke, suddenly remembering that I had left her by herself, something that I must never do. She isn't in the room. A wave of nauseating panic and I am heaving hard. Where is Ah Yoke? I run to the kitchen. No Ah Yoke. I look out into the alley. She's not there either. Hassan is just about to drive off perched at the front of the cart behind Encik Abdullah's buffalo. He looks at me and sees my panic. Where is Ah Yoke, my eyes implore. He looks towards the far end of the alley and I follow his gaze. At the end of the alley, near the communal well, I see a squatting figure playing with some kittens. I run towards the figure.

'Ah Yoke, you silly girl,' I say panting, pinching her hard.

Ah Yoke starts to cry as Hassan pulls away showing me two fingers.

'Ah Lian Jie used to let me play with the kittens,' Ah Yoke howls.

'Hush, Ah Yoke,' I say gently this time, 'you know you can't leave my side.'

'I didn't leave your side Ah Mei Jie,' her voice indignant, 'you left my side and I followed you.'

'Alright, alright, I will never leave you again,' I reassure her. With Ah Yoke by my side, we return home. *What did she see?* But I don't care because my heart is full. Hassan's kiss lingers on my lips as I cross the threshold into my world.

Chapter 13

Lee Household, November 1931 to March 1932

Master Lee's home for good and excitement is seeping from every crack and pore of the old house, and it hasn't stopped since. He arrived in a big boat not long after Mei's arrival. Ah Chin went to collect him at the port. As soon as he stepped into the house, he asked me for a bowl of curry laksa. He told me he's been craving my laksa for months. English food, he said, does not suit his taste, especially the food he was being given at his school. Oh, how that made me smile. It's such a pleasure to serve the young master. He is so different from his father that I wonder if Eminent Mister Lee is the Master's flesh and blood at all. But I shake these impure thoughts away—what am I thinking?

Master Lee, the heir to the Lee shipping fortune, was a tiny dot of blood when I first met him. I knew him before he was even born. Mother was the cook then, and I was her sous chef, helping her chop and cut up ingredients, doing the errands like running over to Encik Abdullah's for oil and spices. It was a lot of work, I remember. When he was born, the whole house celebrated, for he was the long-awaited son and heir. Pity he was not of Eminent Mister Lee's first wife, Number One Madam. She could only bear Lee girls, each dying one after the other except for one, and it was Eminent Mister Lee's second wife who birthed Master Lee. May the Goddess bless her memory. Luckily, Number One Madam takes care of this boy as if he were her own.

'Ah Wan Jie, let's go through the menu,' Number One Madam is in the kitchen, somewhere she hardly steps into, even though the kitchen is every *nyonya's* domain.

'Of course, Madam.'

'What have you got in mind for the dinner party, Ah Wan Jie? You know we will have some important guests—Mr and Mrs Chew of Chew & Sons Imports, Mr and Mrs Tang of C. S. Tang & Sons, and the Tang daughter. You know them. We have a table of eight. Lucky eight, Ah Wan Jie.'

I list the usual Peranakan dishes that the family loves. The Chews and Tangs are Straits Chinese like the Lees and they would be partial to these dishes as well. We've had them for dinners before, so I know that Mrs Chew loves *babi tohay*. Number One Madam gives a nod to that dish because it is also Eminent Mister Lee's favourite. I mentally tick the ingredients list for the *tohay*—*grago* shrimps, fermented red yeast rice, brandy and yeast. I have a jar of tohay fermenting nicely from a month ago, ready to be used to cook this traditional Peranakan dish and I'll have to make more tohay to ferment.

It took Mother a long time to learn how to ferment tohay and it sure did take me much longer to perfect the paste. Chicken buah keluak—that is on the menu too. This is the late Number Two Madam's favourite and she liked the flesh of this poisonous nut, the *buah*, scooped out and mixed with the sauce before being stuffed back into its shell. She had such a craving for it when she was pregnant with Master Lee. Ahhh! The memories—she was a good woman. May the Goddess of Mercy bless her memory. Funny how this strange nut becomes edible after being boiled first and buried in ash after. It does give the dish an earthy after taste. I don't like the taste much, it's like eating dirt, but we eat what we can get as servants. Luckily, chicken buah keluak is also Number One Madam's favourite, so I haven't made a mistake by adding it to be served. And, Master Lee loves laksa. That is of course down on the list. I will have to grate the coconut fresh for the gravy. And the thick rice noodles must be ordered and collected on the same day. I will have to send Ah Mei out for that. We will have chendol for dessert. Since I have to grate the coconut and extract the milk from the desiccated fruit for the laksa gravy, I will keep a potful for the chendol. I'll need to cook the red beans, after soaking them in water overnight, make the agar jelly and order ice from Encik Abdullah. Oh, and there's the palm sugar, what the Peranakans call *gula melaka*, to prepare too. And as I have to make the coconut milk, I thought to add rendang on the list. I remind Number One Madam that Mr Tang adores my rendang.

Check. Check. Check.

Although Number One Madam can cook, she doesn't need to. She is very strict about how I cook, though. Not only do I have to plan the dishes, I must also tell her how I cook them. She gets even more nervous when it is a dinner to impress. I am aware that I mustn't embarrass her. If her face is saved, so will my position. After all, there are so many Hailam cooks these days vying for jobs like mine. These male cooks come from Hainan Island where the men are used to cooking, especially in European man's homes. I must always keep my dishes up to par.

'This is an important dinner, Ah Wan Jie,' my thoughts break like meat falling off a bone with the sound of Number One Madam's voice.

'Yes, Madam, all dinners at the Lee household are important,' I say with pride.

I see a glimmer of gold teeth. Number One Madam nods in approval.

'Ah—also make some five-spiced rolls. Boon loves them and you can't get them in England.'

'Of course, Madam.'

'Ah—I forgot … Master Boon Tong wants us to address him as … uhm … Percy now, by the way. He thinks having an English name would be better for his law career.'

I say Percy out loud and Number One Madam laughs. Don't make his name sound like he's a shit-stirrer, she says. A blush rush over me. I am once more conscious of my Cantonese accent.

'In any case, Master Boon Tong—oh, Master Percy, I mean … will be betrothed. We are proposing marriage to the Tang girl, Siu Lan.'

Wealth marries wealth, was what Mother used to say when she was alive. May the Goddess of Mercy guard her memory. Since Mother's death, the kitchen hasn't been the same. It's lonely cooking on my own. But I would hate to share Mother's secret recipes with anyone. Whatever I've learnt, I've learnt from my mother, who worked her bone to the ground cooking for the Lees.

Mother, your babi tohay recipe will stand in good stead for the dinner. Mother you know how I miss our chats together. I know you'd have done the same thing I had to do with Ah Lian and the baby. What choice did I have, Mother?

The Peranakans are a funny lot. Not all of them are wealthy, this I know. But the wealthy ones stick to one another like flies to rotten meat. They're Chinese but not Chinese. Speak Malay but are not Malay. Eat pork because they're not Muslim and pray to Chinese gods, but act like Europeans. Take Master Lee for example, or should I dare say, Percy. He will take over the family business, something to do with ships, now that he's finished his schooling. He is a smart boy and if I had the money, I would do the same for my son—send him overseas because it's a better education there. But luckily, a celibate and unschooled woman like me has no children or education to worry about. Master Lee speaks English like a native, not that I would understand him. Number One Madam says he studies something called law. The English word sounds like sauce to my Cantonese ear, trying to get used to the Fukien tongue pronouncing English. Well, I know it's not cooking that Master Lee is studying, this much I know. The only Chinese men I know who cook are Hailam. Cooking is women's work after all. Number One Madam says law has to do with the government. Master Lee will have the power to put someone in jail, she had also said. Well, I have nothing to be afraid of. Whatever that thing called law is, he will be good at it, and because he is the Lee son, he will protect me too.

Chapter 14

It is a week after Hassan kissed me. Since that day, we've had a long conversation about our feelings for each other. The words I couldn't say that afternoon in the alleyway came tumbling out of me two days later when Hassan and I met in the back alley again. He didn't know if I was coming or not, he'd said, because I hadn't said yes to him, but he didn't want to miss the chance of showing me how he really feels. So, I found him squatting by the back door waiting for me when I went to empty the chamber pot. He took the smelly pot from me and emptied the contents into the night soil bucket. Then taking my hands, he wiped them using the end of his singlet and smiled at me, melting my heart. The humour he usually displays at his uncle's shop was absent. His voice was serious, his words sincere. I trust Hassan implicitly, now. I know he will never hurt me.

'Hassan-ah! Boy, boy, don't go yet!' Ah Wan Jie calls, sticking her head out of the back door. I blush at the sound of his name and the memory of his fingers stroking my face. The scent of his breath is still fresh in my mind.

'I forgot to order some candlenut. In a hurry to make my rempah. Can Ah Lian go back with you to the shop to buy some. She'll take a rickshaw back.'

I'm about five steps across from the back door, just finished ironing the last of the madam's sarongs and getting ready to take a pile of them to her armoire upstairs when I hear Ah Wan Jie calling out to Hassan. I do my ironing on an old wooden chest at the back of the kitchen. I have to sit on a low stool to iron as the chest only comes up to my knees. It's not the most comfortable position to be in with my knees knocking against the chest and splayed wide apart. But, here, I'm away from the cooking area, so Number One Madam's clothes will not reek of onions and *belachan*, the stinky shrimp paste that the Lees love. My ears prick because Ah Wan Jie has called me by the wrong name.

'Ah Lian?' I ask, confused, looking towards Ah Wan Jie, who pivots around to look at me.

She stumbles on the spot and leans on to the door jamb to steady herself. Ah Wan Jie's face is ashen, making her look sick and ghostly. Her eyes widen in alarm and she starts to mutter something under her breath.

'*Aiya, aiya, choy choy*,' she says, using the Cantonese words to brush off bad luck, at the same time as Hassan steps back into the kitchen. 'I mean, you, Ah Mei, of course. May the Goddess bless Ah Lian's memory.'

Hassan looks over at me and I catch his eye. He seems disturbed by the mention of Ah Lian's name.

'Ah Wan Jie, do I take Ah Yoke with me too?' She needs a wash before dinner and I have much to get on with.' I say this before I start to look too eager to follow Hassan back to Encik Abdullah's.

'Ah Mei, when I ask you to do something, you do it. Ah Yoke can stay with me. Right, Ah Yoke, you stay with Ah Wan Jie while Ah Mei Jie goes out for some *buah keras*. You like rendang too and I will make you a pot of succulent beef rendang, if you're good.

Ah Yoke's face lights up and a trickle of saliva finds its way onto her bib. I step towards her to wipe her mouth but Ah Wan Jie hurries me away.

'Go, go now. And, while you're there, also get me a kilo of dried chillies. I will add them to the fresh ones for a more robust paste.'

'Also, I need more grago shrimp. Did Encik Abdullah get some from the fishermen this morning? You know that making the tohay is not an easy exercise. I am down to last my clay jar. Ha, maybe I'll make some *chinchalok* too.'

'I'll ask my uncle, Ah Wan Jie,' Hassan answers in Malay. His Malay voice is different from his *Hokkien* voice, yet they're from the same person. 'Anything else, *kakak* Wan?'

Ah Wan Jie shoos him away, too busy mentally preparing her dishes. I sigh inwardly at the way Hassan calls Ah Wan Jie kakak, sister, in Malay. This Malay word for sister makes the Hokkien one, jie, sound weak and helpless.

Hassan hurries out the back door beckoning for me to come. I am giddy with excitement and something else I can't name. I pinch myself because I can't believe that I'll be left alone with Hassan, riding on his bullock cart in public. I don't even know if this is allowed. But I don't ask.

Chapter 15

If this is not my portion to meet thee in this life
then let me ever feel that I have missed thy sight
let me not forget for a moment,
let me carry the pangs of this sorrow in my dreams
and in my wakeful hours.

These beautiful words fall from Hassan's lips like a cascading waterfall. I sit next to him, my heart pounding quickly. We are so close, I'm sure he can hear the beats too.

'Mei, let me say sorry again … about that day … the kiss … I didn't mean to disrespect you … I mean to say, I respect you … I want to be with you, Mei. I really like you, Mei … a lot.'

I am tongue-tied. Is there an appropriate response to this?

Yes, there is. I like you too. Maybe even I love you.

What does a girl say or do in male company? Especially in the company of a young man who is not from her race?

She should just be herself. Say what's on her mind. Love doesn't see colour nor creeds.

But, I stay silent.

Hassan glances over quickly and our eyes meet for a couple of seconds. I turn away as he starts to drive the bullock cart back to his uncle's shop. Eyes on the road ahead, he repeated the words of the song he recited earlier.

'Rabindranath Tagore, Mei. He taught me those words. Tagore is India's most talented poet. I want to be like him when I grow up.'

'How did you learn to read, Hassan?' I finally find my tongue.

'Before my parents died, I went to school in India. There I learnt some English, some Bengali, my mother tongue.'

Hassan's parents are no longer alive. The same ache I felt in my chest when I realized that I will never see Ma or Ah Mah and Huat again find its way to my throat and form a teary lump there. I swallow back my tears and look ahead.

'After they died, I was sent to live with my uncle, Abdullah. He's a kind man but doesn't understand why I like reading and poetry … just wants me to help him in his shop and fan him. He keeps telling people that I am his *punkawallah*. That's why he keeps asking me to fan him. How ridiculous.' Hassan looks at me and laughs. The vision of Hassan fanning Encik Abdullah made me laugh too. We chuckle together and I start to feel at ease.

'I mean I don't mind fanning him but I am hardly a punkawallah … anyway … it is what it is. I'm glad for a roof over my head and food in my stomach. At least, he's kind enough to pay me a small salary too.'

With that, Hassan stops the bullock cart by a food stall and jumps off.

'Hold this.' He passes me the rope attached to the buffaloes. 'Pull tight if they move.'

Before I can ask *where are you going*, Hassan disappears into the dusky light and heads behind a tree. A sense of panic engulfs me. I look towards the spot where I last saw Hassan. A familiar face greets me—the man with the cloudy glass eye. He looks intently at me. He slides towards me. But mid-way, he turns and walks away.

Hassan appears from behind the tree and goes towards the food stall. I see him chat with the stall owner before picking up a packet. I am instantly flooded with relief. The fear of seeing the glassy-eyed man dissipates and I soon forget about him.

'*Roti* John, Mei.' He hands me half of the food before climbing back up on the cart. He settles back down next to me, takes the rope from me with his free hand, and bites into his half of the food.

I have never seen anything like this before. An omelette sandwiched between two slices of sharp-headed bread, the ones that Master Lee likes with his chicken curry.

'This is a pure genius of an invention, Mei,' Hassan says between mouthfuls while gesturing at me to take a bite of mine, 'it's simply roti, you know the long roti … anyway, it's a sandwich named after a Mat Salih called John, stuffed with curried minced lamb, omelette, and lots of chilli sauce.'

I take a sniff at my Roti John. I wonder who the Mat Salih, the Malay word for *ang moh*, named John was. Was he British, American or European? Did he have red hair as the Fukien name, ang moh, for his race suggests? Mrs Smith has yellow hair and so does Mr Smith, although his hair colour is slightly darker than his wife's. Yet they're still called ang moh kwee, red hair devils. Their children don't have red coloured hair either, although their son is named John. And they aren't devils at all. In fact, they are the kindest people I've ever known. Mrs Smith always gives me food to take home and whenever there are jobs that the other ladies in her temple wanted done, she'd give them to me. She calls her temple church. She tells me that her God is a good god, a loving one, whom she calls Father. I don't say anything because Guanyin Goddess is just as good and Mother Mazu, who Uncle Cheong prays to, is just as benevolent.

My life working for Mrs Smith seems so long ago now.

Onions, garlic, and cumin stream into my nostrils. I take a bite and taste green chillies, minced meat and a savoury-sweet chilli sauce. The green chillies leave a tingling heat on my lips and tongue, making me salivate. I am getting used to spicy food because at the Lee house, every dish seems to be spicy. Sometimes, I do crave for a simple bowl of white rice and a fried egg like what we used to eat at home when food was scarce. But then, I remember that home is the Lee house now. And although food is no longer scarce, beggars cannot be choosers.

'Good, right, huh, huh?' Hassan says, his cheeks puffed with this delicious food, his eyes twinkling. He eats with his right hand, driving the bull cart with his left.

I nod and take another happy bite of my Roti John. The bulls seem contented too as they lumber back to Encik Abdullah's.

'Who is Ah Lian, Hassan?' I ask, finishing my last bite and mopping my mouth with the back of my hand.

Hassan gulps down his final mouthful. The bulls stop moving.

'Why you ask me this, Mei?' I hear a hesitance in his answer.

'Nothing, it's just that Ah Wan Jie seems scared of Ah Lian and when she said her name earlier, she went pale.'

Hassan sighs.

'Ah Lian used to be a servant girl like you.'

'I know that. Ah Wan Jie has told me that she used to look after Ah Yoke.'

'Yes, but she made a big mistake.'

'What?'

'Nothing, Mei. Let's not talk about it, ok. You won't be making the same mistake, I know. I won't let you. I won't let them hurt you. I won't let them get away with it.'

Don't let them get away with it.

The voice in my head hisses.

I hear the urgency in Hassan's voice. I don't probe. The truth will surface soon enough if this is how Fate wants to play her cards. I whisper a prayer to quieten the voice.

Then, Hassan says, 'Mei, Ah Lian's is not my story to tell. Let's leave her memory to rest.'

After telling me this, he tugs at the bulls and we move on again. We arrive at Encik Abdullah's shop and I buy Ah Wan Jie her candlenuts and dried chillies. Encik Abdullah is in a good mood and packs a bunch of coriander and spring onions into my shopping bag.

'Tell Kakak Wan that her grago shrimps will be available soon.'

I hop on the rickshaw that will take me home, my mind on a servant girl named Ah Lian.

Chapter 16

The November mid-morning sun is blazing as I put the washing out to dry. Number One Madam had recently added washing to my list of chores even though looking after Ah Yoke is still my priority. My responsibility for the laundry started after the Eminent Mister Lee's grand birthday in October.

Number One Madam only wants me to wash her clothes, Ah Wan Jie said. Number One Madam had asked her to inform me. I found this to be very odd. Number One Madam could've told me herself, then I could've met her. But I kept this thought to myself.

'Do you know why, Ah Wan Jie?'

Ah Wan Jie didn't know. She could only tell me that the Malay washer-woman, Nur, will continue to wash and iron the rest of everyone's. Nur must be relieved to know she has one less person's clothes to wash, I thought to myself.

Ah Yoke loves playing with the water as I wash the madam's laundry. The chore takes up three whole days of my time. Number One Madam changes twice a day—she wears one sarong in the morning and a different one in the evening. And if she has to entertain or go out, she changes more than twice. So, I have quite a bit to wash and if I time it right, I can usually hang the clothes out by mid-morning when the sun is getting hot and by the evening, I'll have a fresh pile of laundry to iron. It's not easy to see if the creases have been ironed out in the dim dusky light, but I try my best. Number One Madam's batik sarongs don't give me much trouble. It's her delicate blouses with the intricate needlework that I'm afraid to spoil. I found a workaround by ironing those last when the charcoal iron is not as hot anymore.

The gardener Chandra has just finished pruning the bougainvillea bushes not far from the washing area. He is picking up the pink petals and leaves to be burnt at the back of the garden and Ah Yoke is helping him. I know that I shouldn't let her out of my sight, but I trust that Chandra won't let anything bad happen to the Elder Lee daughter, and it's good that Ah Yoke has something fun to do. The Lee house never ceases to buzz with activity. There are always people about—business associates of Eminent Mister Lee, Number One Madam's mahjong friends, and the other wives' visitors and friends. And let's not forget the workmen like Chandra and Chin the driver. Number One Madam has her own rickshaw puller and so do the other wives. They squat outside the iron gate waiting to be instructed and sometimes, I see Ah Wan Jie bringing them a flask of water or a tiffin of food.

When the workmen are out at the back, the mui tsai are told to stay away. That means no using the outdoor toilet because that is used only by the men. If we need more water, a water carrier ferries buckets to the house from the pump at the end of the road, even though the Lee family has a well in their garden. The Lees have their own water carrier, a young boy about fourteen years old. As the Lee house is a mansion, so large that an army of servants and workmen are always needed to run the place, it is possible that the servants never see one another at all. Number One Madam has two of her own female servants—one mui tsai and one Black and White Amah. The mui tsai, named Ah Poh, sleeps on the floor outside Number One Madam's room and is at Madam's beck and call during the night, especially when she needs the chamber pot. Ah Ping Yee, who wears a black trouser and white blouse, has a mattress in the servant's quarters near the outhouse. In fact, Ah Wan Jie and Ah Ping Yee used to share the room at the back of the kitchen where I sleep now.

Ah Ping Yee is the only servant who is allowed to leave the house. She has a room that she rents in a boarding house for female servants from China. Ah Ping Yee has sworn to remain celibate and not to take a husband as long as she is out of China. She had explained to Ah Wan Jie, who tells me, that for a woman like Ah Ping Yee, the reason for leaving China is to send money home, so being married would mean a loss of income for her family.

'You know, Ping-chieh, probably has a husband at home,' Ah Wan Jie confided in me, 'who needs her to send money home. Men can be so useless sometimes.'

Ah Wan Jie also said that Ah Ping Yee (whom she calls Ping-chieh, Sister Ping, in Cantonese) was not alone; there are many women like her and they can be recognized by the way they style their hair—all pulled back and knotted into a chignon. Each woman had to be initiated into spinsterhood by going through an ancient hair-combing ritual. I like Ah Ping Yee. She's like an aunt to me and I have great respect for her. What a loss of an opportunity to find love and have a family of one's own. Life is so unfair sometimes.

'Yes, life can be unfair,' Ah Wan Jie said, reading my thoughts, 'but what they lose out on they transfer to the children they look after. Look at Master Lee. It was Ping-chieh who loved and doted on him. And … '

'And what, Ah Wan Jie?'

'Never mind, nothing important. It's because Ping-chieh had suckled Master when he was a baby that Number One Madam refuses to let her go. She came to the Lee house shortly after leaving China.'

Ah Wan Jie had a faraway look in her eyes as soon as she finished her sentence. After that intimate sharing, she shrugged her shoulders and let out a long and deep sigh.

While the women of the house have their personal help, the men like Eminent Mister Lee and the young master have their own. Eminent Mister Lee has a punkawallah and a house boy to take care of his needs. And Master Lee has his own house boy. It's curious that these house boys are actually men. I don't know why they're still referred to as boys. Perhaps they started work when they were boys. Apart from boy servants, both Eminent Mister and Master Lee share a motor car which is driven by Ah Chin. Chin's main job is to drive the Lee men around, wash and polish the car.

As Eminent Mister Lee has two other wives, the little wives have their own entourage of servants. What a full house the Lee household is.

* * *

I am hanging one of Number One Madam's blouses on the bamboo pole when I see the young master striding my way with a big smile on his face.

'Hello,' he greets me with his hand extended, 'I'm Percy Lee.' His Cantonese has a hint of the Fukienese inflection.

This is the first time I am meeting the young master and I am not expecting to be greeted this way. I drop the bamboo pole not because I want to shake his hand, but because I am taken aback by his casual manners so much so that I am unsure of what I am meant to do. I bend down to pick it up. He does the same and we end up holding the bamboo clothes hanger, he on one end and me on the other, with his mother's blouse hanging in the middle. It is not a long bamboo pole; Percy Lee and I are close enough that I can smell fresh talc. My throat feels parched.

'Master Lee … good morning,' I croak.

The awkwardness is painfully visible. And I keep my eyes downcast because I don't think it's right to look at one's master in the eye.

I feel his smile through his words. He says that I have nothing to be afraid of. He also says something, which I've never heard before—that all humans are equal and that I am to call him Percy.

'*Boon gor, Boon gor,*' Ah Yoke runs up to us. I see Chandra watching her from a distance, mindful that he needs to keep an eye on the Lee daughter. He goes back to pruning the bougainvillea hedges again once Ah Yoke is safely by Percy Lee's side. The excitement in her voice is loud and clear. I don't know why she insists on calling him Big Brother Boon, even though he is younger than her by a couple of years. I wonder if her simple ways and mind make Number One Madam and Eminent Mister Lee think she is younger. Maybe, they don't want people to know that the first-born Lee is a daughter and one who is not like other girls. There are too many maybes.

'Po Gek, there you are!' Percy Lee greets his sister fondly. His love for her is palpable—he wears it on his face. 'I was looking for you. Mother said that you're in the kitchen, where you usually are.'

Ah Yoke gives Percy Lee a big hug and clings to him like how Huat used to glue himself to me when he's happy or when he needed some comforting. She is slightly shorter than her brother.

'Flower for you,' Ah Yoke says, thrusting a bunch of dark pink petals in Percy Lee's face.

'Thank you,' he says with a chuckle, stepping back to take the flowers. 'How about we take a walk into town? Go buy some nice *kuih-kuih* for dessert later. Father likes those red tortoises filled with sweet mung bean paste. *Ang Gu Kuih.*'

'I like them too, gor,' Ah Yoke says, catching a dribble with her bib just in time.

I beam with pride. She's getting to be quite good at cleaning up after herself and I didn't even have to signal her with our code. Huat would be good at cleaning up after himself too, I assure myself. I push the thoughts of my brother to the corners of my mind.

'Yes, of course, you do.' There is generosity in Percy Lee's voice. He tugs gently at one of Ah Yoke's plaits and laughs, a kind gentle laugh.

'You know, I'm glad that Mother agreed to allow you out. You're much better for it,' Percy Lee tells his sister. Then he turns to me and says, 'Mei, I'd like you to come too. I'm sure Po Gek would love you to.'

'Yes, yes, Mei Jie, come come.'

The flesh of Ah Yoke's hanging upper lip quivers with emotion. I know her well enough now to know that she is both happy and afraid. She is probably scared that I won't be allowed to go with her, to protect her, and we've never been to town before. And she's happy that her big brother is back home from overseas—she's said so many times. The gap in her upper lip glistens with saliva and I make a gesture with my hand to tell her to wipe her lips again. She picks up her bib—the one with a red peony—and dabs them. I nod at her and she looks at me, imploring.

'As long as Number One Madam is fine with you taking Elder Daughter into town and my chaperoning, it is my duty to come.'

'Of course she'll be fine with it,' Percy Lee affirms, 'you're with me and accompanying the Elder Daughter of the Lee house—what can be more appropriate than that?'

Percy Lee says this with broad assurance and a confidence that I wish I knew.

Ah Yoke hugs me in excitement and I almost fall backwards from the force of her embrace. Just then, a magpie lands on the bamboo pole and sits like a clothes peg on Number One Madam's blouse. It looks at me intently and opens its mouth letting out a warbled but sweet melody. A magpie is a sign of good fortune, Ah Mah used to tell me and I mustn't shoo it away. The song finished, the bird lifts its black and white wings and flies off into the mid-morning sky.

It seems that nobody but me has noticed this little bird.

'Come, Ah Mei-jie, let's go.'

I pat my hair into place and straighten my samfoo. Maybe it's a good day to wear my kasut manek again, but Ah Wan Jie's voice puts a stop to this fantasy.

Best put it away, you won't need them here.

Chapter 17

When Ah Mei asked me for permission to take Ah Yoke into town accompanied by the young master, I was surprised. It was the young master's wish, she had said. I was even more surprised on hearing this. Master Lee wanting to take his sister into town and asking the mui tsai to tag along—that is something I've never witnessed ever. Studying far away from home, living amongst so many *kwailo* must be the reason for his absurd behaviour. These foreign ghosts must have influenced him, making him forget who he is. He's only been back a few months, in fact, during the Ghost Month itself, about ten days after Ah Mei's arrival, and he is already behaving differently to what is expected of him. He is like a boat with no rudder. Has he forgotten the conventions? I am horrified remembering when Master Lee returned. Perhaps, he is possessed. Nobody should travel during the month of the dead. *May Guanyin Goddess bless his soul.*

I don't know Ah Mei to be a liar, she has been honest with me as far as I know, so in a way, I took her word for it. To be frank, I was too distracted about the menu for dinner to entertain the thought about the inappropriateness of it all. I am also busy preparing the tohay for the important dinner coming up in a month's time. Tohay needs this long to ferment. Actually, the longer the better. I am too busy to mind about conventions or rules at the moment. As long as Master Lee is in charge, what more can I say or do?

'Make sure that Ah Yoke doesn't run off,' I cautioned Mei, 'it's town, not the market, where she is used to going.'

I've noticed a glow in Ah Mei's face recently, which wasn't there before. I hear her mumbling to herself every now and then when she's washing or ironing or mending Number One Madam's clothes. And every now and then, her lips break into a slight smile as she pulls the needle and thread through one of Madam's delicate lace blouses.

'What are these sounds you're making, Mei?'

'Oh, nothing, Ah Wan Jie,' she would reply hesitantly.

With some prodding, she finally told me that they're sounds of letters.

Yum Gong, goodness gracious, what is the world coming to—a servant girl making the sounds of letters? I did wonder who was she learning this from but frankly, as long as she keeps her body to herself, and not make a mistake like many mui tsai do, I wash my hands off Ah Mei's case. Don't I already have enough of a burden looking after Ah Lian's soul?

These thoughts flutter through my mind when Hassan arrives with the groceries. Bags of onions, garlic and dried shrimps.

'Kakak Wan, *selamat pagi*, good morning,' he greets me, always politely referring to me as big sister in Malay. 'Your goods.'

He bows theatrically and casts his eyes around furtively as if looking for something.

I wonder if he is looking for some treasure to steal. The only precious thing in my kitchen is the Kitchen God's altar. A Muslim would not be interested in that.

'Mei is with the Elder princess?'

'Where would she be, Hassan, ha?'

Hassan laughs. He has a good nature, this boy.

'*Adoi, saya bodoh*—I am stupid. Of course.'

He arranges the bags on the floor near the pounding station by the *batu lesong*, where I blend all my rempahs. I have already prepared the rest of the ingredients to make the chilli paste that would fragrant the curries that I'll be serving later.

Before Hassan leaves, he gives the kitchen another look around.

This makes me wonder could it be Hassan who has been helping Ah Mei sound out the English alphabet. I know he speaks English. Encik Abdullah told me this himself. I also know that Hassan loves to read. So, I wouldn't put it past that boy to be the one teaching Ah Mei the sounds of English words ...

... which can only mean one thing—they have been spending time together.

And, his curious glances around the kitchen on delivery days tell me that he is looking for something. His inquisitive questions about Mei indicate a personal interest.

She's the treasure he's looking for.

Chapter 18

Percy Lee is at least a head and half taller than me. I am not short by Chinese standards. Ah Pa has long bones and I take after him. As I walk beside him, the talc I detected earlier catches in my throat again and I detect another flavour on the body of Percy Lee. It smells spicy and fresh.

Ah Yoke walks beside me because I have to hold her hand. To the other pedestrians we must look quite a sight—three people in a row shaded by a paper parasol that the mui tsai at the centre is holding. I try my best to shade both Ah Yoke and Percy Lee. To do this, I have to raise my right hand higher than usual, while my left hand holds onto Ah Yoke's right. The sun is piercing now. The paper parasol emits a unique smell that reminds me of rotting bark.

I notice that Percy Lee is several shades browner than his sister. It could be that they're from the wombs of different women. Ah Wan Jie had said once that the late Number Two Madam, Percy Lee's biological mother, was of mixed-blood. She had come from a long and entrenched line of Straits

Chinese who can claim a Malay relative or two in their lineage. Number One Madam is a *sinkeh*, a new arrival, from China, who had been brought to Nanyang at seventeen from Eminent Mister Lee's ancestral village in Swatow to marry him. She was not high-born, according to Ah Wan Jie, but not of peasant stock either. Ah Wan Jie thinks that Number One Madam is the daughter of a mercantile family, a class of people frowned upon by Confucius scholars. As a sinkeh, it was imperative that she finds ways to fit in.

'Tell me about yourself, Mei.'

Percy Lee's question interrupts my thoughts and stumps me. What is there to say? I am a lowly servant girl and he is the heir of the Lee shipping fortune and business.

'I … er … I …'

'It's ok, Mei, don't be shy. Ok, tell you what, let me start. I am Percival Lee Boon Tong. My friends call me Percy. Mother and Father call me Boon Tong,' he laughs as he says this, 'see, not so hard. You are … ?'

'Lim Mei Mei.'

That is all I can muster. I don't want to talk about Ma and Ah Pa because I am afraid that I might cry just remembering them, especially Ma. I wonder how Huat is doing and how is Ah Mah coping with her shoulder pain.

'Mei Mei means very beautiful,' Percy Lee offers an explanation of my name. 'It's a beautiful name, Mei. A name that matches a face in every sense of the word.'

I nod awkwardly, tongue-tied while a prickly heat rises from my stomach to my face. What am I to say to that?

'Mei-jie, gor like you.'

I tighten my hold of Ah Yoke's hand as a warning for her to stop.

Ow. I loosen my grip.

'Yes, you're right, Po Gek, gor does like Ah Mei.'

My cheeks are hot with embarrassment. What do I say to that? Do? Think?

Percy Lee lets out a good-natured laugh and apologizes for teasing Ah Yoke and me.

'But Mei also means little sister, Po Gek,' Percy Lee says, 'and I care for Ah Mei like she is my little sister.' He grins at me, adding another layer to my embarrassment. Ah Yoke nods, flashing me a smile.

'I'm interested to know, Mei, how did you come to live with us. You see, at law school in London, we had studied the Slavery Abolition Act of 1833. It's the law that freed men and women from being slaves in the Empire. Do you know what I am talking about, Mei?'

I shake my head. What are slaves? Is it another type of servant? I don't say anything because what is there to say?

'Right. I think that indentured servitude is a type of slavery and I want to help put a stop to this. There is a law in Malaya—'

Percy Lee prattles on methodically, as if he is giving me a lesson. I have no idea what he is talking about regarding some new law that is related to mui tsai. I stare ahead and wish Hassan was here instead because he and I would have more things to talk about. I would be able to hear him recite some Tagore and he would show me how to make the sounds of the letters that form words. And, I would be able to recount the stories that Ah Mah used to tell me, especially the one about the star-crossed lovers who were united by a magpie bridge. Hassan loves that fairytale. He says that he is the Cowherd and I am his Weaver Girl.

My lips are curling into a smile when they fall again to Percy Lee's question.

'So how did you come to live with us?'

'Master Lee ... I ... I ... a messenger boy named Ban Guan came to fetch me at my home one day ... and I have been at your house now ... nearly four months,' I give Percy Lee the best answer I could think of, the words tumbling out quickly.

'Look gor, ting ting sweets. I want, I want,' Ah Yoke pulls her hand away and runs towards the itinerant sweet vendor.

'Ah Yoke!' I call and run after her, throwing the parasol on the path.

Just as well that the old ting-ting sweet uncle is not far off. A circle of children with their mui tsai are already there. I see Ah Yoke push a girl aside so she could get to the front of the sweet seller. He is hard at work chipping away at a white slab of candy. Ting. Ting. Ting. We have no other name for this hard candy that sticks to your palette eased only by the heat of your mouth as it melts into a milky goodness. I've only tried it once when Ma brought a piece home. Her madam had given her one sliver for me and Huat. With Ma's dexterous knife skills, we managed to divide one small piece of candy the size of a thumb of ginger into four chips. My heart burns as I see Ah Mah's toothless grin once more. It was a happy day.

'Ah Yoke, don't push,' I remind her gently pulling her away from the front, 'wait for your turn.'

Percy Lee strides up with the parasol now closed. I reach out for it but he gestures for me to stop, tells me it's ok he'll hold it. Then, he hands me some money and tells me to treat myself and his sister.

Amidst the ting-tinging sounds of the sweet uncle chiselling away, the street is buzzing with human chatter. I see a couple of mui tsai look at me suspiciously. I don't hold their gaze. Percy Lee approaches one of them. I recognize her from Encik Abdullah's shop. She lives on the next street over and her family are merchants with a small shop in Chinatown on Telok Ayer Road.

'Hello, I'm Percy Lee, son of Lee Guang Hoe. Don't be afraid, I just want to ask you something.'

I couldn't help but shake my head internally. What was Percy Lee doing? Why does he think that just because he opens his mouth to ask us something, we would open our mouths to answer him.

The mui tsai, Ah Cheng, shrinks and takes a step back, bewilderment dotted across her eyes.

'Master Lee, our sweets are ready,' I say rescuing poor Ah Cheng from the pain of her dilemma.

'Gor ... gor, come.' Ah Yoke drags her brother away as Ah Cheng and I exchange a look.

Chapter 19

Singapore Town, Year of the Monkey, 1932

The kitchen is filled with the aromatic scents of spices yet again. The heaty fumes of the rempah is cooled by the moisture in the air. Fat monsoon rain drops drum on the tiles in the air well while water jars collect rain water. A cacophony of pelting and frying. These are sounds that I have grown used to. Ah Wan Jie needs my help, so I set Ah Yoke up in her activity corner at the end of the kitchen. There, she can draw on the cement floor. She is getting quite good at drawing with pieces of charcoal that I've salvaged from Ah Wan Jie's stock. Sometimes Hassan gives me a couple of carbon chunks for Ah Yoke to doodle with. I leave a platter of love letters, those left over from the Chinese New Year, for Ah Yoke to snack on before I leave her to her art work. We are already eighteen days into this auspicious year. The Lees celebrated the first fifteen days of the new year with a big feast on *chap gor meh*, the fifteenth night. We are now properly into the year of the Water Monkey.

'I'll be back when the cooking is done, Yoke, keep on drawing those lovely flowers.' Ah Yoke looks up and grins at me, then continues with her work.

Ah Wan Jie is frying up some chilli paste when I join her in the cooking area. I finish grinding up some more rempah using the batu lesong like how she had shown me. This type of pestle and mortar requires a lot of wrist work in the pressing and rolling of the ingredients on a stone slab with a cylindrical stone pestle. Ah Wan Jie's joints are swollen again and the rainy season is making her arthritis worse. While the rains have been a good sign for the new Monkey year, it is not a good tiding for wind-trapped bones. The granite pestle and mortar is turning out a wet and rather course paste made of chillies, shallots, lemon grass, candlenut, garlic, ginger and galangal. My hands are aching too as I scrape the paste up to be used later, so I can imagine how much worse it would be for Ah Wan Jie. A pungent aroma perfumes the air as another batch of rempah cooks in hot oil. I take over the stirring from Ah Wan Jie as she sits back down to rest. The paste frying in hot oil is so spicy that my eyes start to water and my nose tickles from the fumes. I add the cubes of beef into the hot chilli oil mix and give it a good stir, and allow the meat to stew in its juices for a bit. Ah Wan Jie is making beef rendang. The secret ingredient in this curry is fresh coconut milk, she said. In fact, Peranakan curries are cooked mostly with coconut milk, I've discovered. Ah Wan Jie's coconut milk is creamy and thick. She told me that she learned the method of squeezing milk from grated coconut from her mother, who learned it from a Malay woman in their kampung. Ah Wan Jie makes a fresh pot every morning. I give the pot of coconut milk a good stir before pouring it into the wok. The beef will now stew in the copper-orange curry sauce infused with coconut milk on a low fire for a couple of hours until tender. I've grown to like this dish. I think the secret ingredient is the toasted coconut that's added at the end of the simmering process. Ah Wan Jie calls the toasted coconut *kerisik*. So I toast the desiccated coconut in a dry pan in preparation for this.

Ah Wan Jie is on her feet again. She hasn't had time to warm her wooden stool because there are just too many things to do today.

'You remember the Tang daughter is coming for dinner tonight,' Ah Wan Jie reminds me as she stirs another pot, this one filled with chicken and potatoes in a thick yellow coconut-based curry sauce. She adds in a generous amount of salt and puts the lid on, leaving the curry to simmer a little longer. 'The dinner that should've happened last year. Number One Madam made such a fuss about it, remember? And then didn't bother to tell me why she cancelled it.'

'Yes, I remember. What's the Tang daughter's favourite dish?' I ask, piqued to know what the Tang daughter likes to eat since there's a dish each pandering to everyone's desires.

'Number One Madam did not say,' Ah Wan Jie says casually, without looking at me. 'A Peranakan girl is taught to cook more than to enjoy what she cooks. Even though she is taught to cook, Mei, once she is married, she will not be cooking, especially if she's marrying into a household like the Lee's.'

I let that information soak in. Percy Lee is getting married.

* * *

Ah Yoke is peeking through the latticed panel that divides the living room from the Guest Hall. The Guest Hall, which Ah Wan Jie calls the tia besar, is the belly of the house where important guests are waited upon and served by Number One Madam's mui tsai, Ah Poh, and Ah Wan Jie during a big party.

The partition, made of redwood carved with intricate scenes from the Analects of Confucius, acts as a privacy barrier shielding the guests from the family quarters. Just in front of the latticed panel is an altar to Guan Gong, the patron god of brotherhood, and if you position yourself well, you can spy on the guests without them seeing you.

'Ah Yoke, come away,' I whisper urgently to her, 'you mustn't be seen.'

'Boon gor is there, I want to go in and join him.'

'No, Ah Yoke, you know the rules.'

Ah Yoke knows the rules—she has to stay out of sight. She's hidden many times behind the screen spying on her father and his business associates. It's a game she plays. One day when I thought I'd lost her, I found her there observing her step-mother, Number Two Madam, entertaining her guests, a bevy of ladies from the same type of temple like Mrs Smith's. They gather there every Wednesday morning to read the book that Mrs Smith has as well. They also call it the Bible. Ah Yoke loves to listen to the stories from this book. One lady would read in English, another would translate the story into Malay. The ladies would then ask each other questions and answer these questions amongst themselves. The language that Number Two Madam speaks with her visitors is Malay mixed with Fukien with some English thrown in. I don't understand everything because my Malay is not so good. But I understand Fukienese and some English words like water, sea, and red. Hassan has been teaching me some English, that's how I know.

Number Two Madam was actually Number Three Madam. She rose up in wifely rank when Number Two Madam passed away soon after Percy Lee was born. Eminent Mister Lee was considering marrying another woman when Number Three Madam gave birth to a son. Percy Lee and Ah Yoke have a half-brother named Joseph Lee Boon Heng. He is now about two, and I heard, small and sickly. As I don't serve the new Number Two Madam, I don't get to see her or her baby son very much. Another Black and White servant, a *majie*, looks after the infant and the rest of her children—two girls—who are four and six. Their Black and White servant is a friend of Ah Ping Yee and she is the one who tells Ah Ping Yee everything that is going on in the new Number Two Madam's quarters. Ah Wan Jie gets her news third hand this way.

I am torn between shepherding Ah Yoke away from the party and spying on what's happening as well. I am curious too but I don't want to seem eager in front of Ah Yoke.

'I want to know who will be gor's wife and if he like her or not,' Ah Yoke says, echoing my thoughts.

Chapter 20

The guests arrive and the silence is now filled with chatter, compliments and laughter. Mr and Mrs Tang and their daughter Siu Lan sparkle from all the jewellery that they're wearing. Mrs Tang is wearing the most beautiful gold *kerosang*, a brooch that fastens the front of her *kebaya*, a typical nyonya's blouse. The diamonds that stud her six-point star brooch shimmer under the crystal chandelier, the biggest piece of jewellery in the Guest Hall. Miss Siu Lan is wearing a similar kebaya except for her sparkling silver kerosang, which was shaped to symbolize a mother and two children, studded with diamonds. Mrs Chew praises Siu Lan for this symbolic choice of jewellery. Mr and Mrs Chew are less ostentatious, even though Mrs Chew's sarong kebaya is exquisitely tailored. Mrs Chew is, however, more talkative than her husband, and I much prefer her over Mrs Tang.

'Come, come, sit, sit.' Everyone takes their place around the table as Number One Madam gestures to the places where she wants her guests to sit.

Ah Yoke watches the scene with intense concentration. I am surprised that she can hold herself this long without fidgeting, something that she usually does when standing still. Like her, I am also mesmerized by the elegance and pomposity of the show taking place before my eyes.

Lots of exaggerated praises are passed. Kind words fall from the mouths of these distinguished guests so freely but they echo hollow.

Oh what a good looking man Percy Lee is.

How clever he is—a lawyer, is it?

Eminent Mister Lee must be so proud to have such a filial son and heir to his shipping dynasty.

Meanwhile, the Tang daughter sits there without lifting her head.

'It is rather unusual for the groom to be meeting the bride,' Mr Tang says, his voice stiff, officious, 'you must know that we are a modern family. So I have permitted this strange request.'

'Aiya, Mister Tang, we thank you for your generosity,' Number One Madam says, 'you know, our son Percy, is a modern man. A modern man fit for a modern family like yours.'

There is an empty coldness to her words. This is the first time I'm seeing Number One Madam up close. Her face is pulled back tightly by a low bun and she has a large forehead with a mole on her left temple. Her sarong kebaya outshines the other two nyonya by miles. And her diamond brooch iridescent, sparkling like a big star, is brighter than Mrs Tang's.

'Thank you, Mister Tang for acquiescing to my request.' Percy Lee's warm laugh and words melt his mother's icy phrases. The back of Percy Lee's head bobs as he laughs.

'I have every intention to honour your daughter, as Mr and Mrs Chew will witness. I wanted for Siu Lan to meet me in an open and safe space. I couldn't think of a better place than my home, which will soon be Siu Lan's too.'

On these words, Siu Lan lifts her head and gives Percy Lee a wan smile. I detect gratitude in the slight curvature of her lips. Her head lowers again when Mrs Tang gives a little cough.

The next voice I hear is Mrs Chew's. Her profile shows a sagging chin and an ample bosom. 'Wah, wah, how generous the young master is. If only my daughters were still unmarried. What I won't do to jump at a chance like this?' she says, chuckling in over-the-top mirth.

'Well … ' it is Eminent Mister Lee's turn to speak, 'well … this is a joyous occasion. Of course, we must still consult with the matchmaker to set an auspicious date.' His voice is business-like and transactional.

'Of course, of course, one must not shirk one's traditions even if one embraces modernity,' Mr Tang says, his tone serious.

'You are right, Tang Yong Ban, you are right,' Eminent Mister Lee says, standing up to face Mr Tang and raising his brandy goblet to him. 'And, my ships and tankers, your carriages and cars will merge in this marriage to form the Lee & Tang Tanker & Carriage Company, starting a new tradition.'

'Let us celebrate this Water Monkey Year in the Gregorian year of 1932. Two great families will merge and become one,' Mr Tang adds.

At that, the two men clink glasses and down a shot of brandy in celebration.

The two soon-to-be related nyonya murmur in exaggerated excitement. With everyone beaming, Number One Madam rings a silver bell and Ah Poh shuffles in with a tray of tea, nuts and tidbits.

'Come, come, let's have some tea and munchies before dinner is served.' Number One Madam says with a ring of authority in her voice.

Chapter 21

I manage to prise Ah Yoke gently away from the scene taking place behind the screen. It's time for her bath. I am eager to get her to bed as soon as possible.

The Lee family's bathhouse is the size of a little cottage attached to the main house. It is north-facing, the cardinal direction which ensures Heavenly protection and fortuity. Because this good luck direction must always be energized allowing a continuous flow of blessings, the feng shui master advises that the bathhouse be decorated with luscious verdant plants that Chandra has to take care of everyday. He is not allowed to let the plants turn brown or die off. A ceramic Shanghai tub, greenish-brown in colour, with an ornate coiling five-clawed dragon, sits in the middle of the square bathhouse. The bathhouse has an opening at the centre of its ceiling so that rain water, a natural element, can flow from the outside in. Reflected on the water's surface is the open sky, again inviting nature in. This water tub represents the lake, a body of water symbolizing wealth.

Ah Yoke sits, naked, on the low stool by the Shanghai tub. The tub is filled to the brim. It has been an exceptionally rainy February. There's a slight chill in the air because of the northeasterly winds blowing at this time of year. This evening, the dusky sky is streaked with ribbons of clouds like dough crullers reflecting back at me from the urn.

'One, two, three,' I say, pouring a bucket of water over Ah Yoke's head which comes up to my stomach.

She squeals in shock and inhales deeply as the cold water hits her. I do this again three times until her body is used to the water's temperature. I rub the bar of jasmine-scented soap on her wet head until it lathers. Then, I wash her hair. Her eyes are closed like Huat's was when I used to wash his hair by the communal pump. Ah Yoke's skin is pale compared to mine. It has a yellow tint, the colour of tofu. Her hair is thick and long and it takes me a while to get all of it soaped and rinsed. When I am done, I pass the soap to her and she washes between her legs like I'd shown her how. I remember the first time I bathed Ah Yoke and my surprise in discovering that nobody had ever showed her how to wash herself properly. No wonder she was always complaining of pain when urinating. The complaints are lesser now and washing between her legs has become natural to her.

* * *

I wait for Ah Yoke to fall asleep before I leave her room. I turn the key locking her in. These are my instructions because like Aunty Eng, Ah Yoke walks in her sleep. Ah Lian used to sleep in Ah Yoke's room, but Number One Madam changed the rules when I arrived. The floorboards creak as I make my way back to the servant's quarters. The house is huge and I must walk along the corridor past Number One Madam's room and then further along past Eminent Mister Lee's chambers before I get to the grand stairs that will take me down to the servant's exit door.

Night has set in. The house is glowing, light emanating from the candles along the upstairs corridor and from the Lee surname lanterns that hang at the front of the house. The pair is lit tonight to indicate the presence of important guests. With the windows wide open and the upper floors immersed in semi-darkness, I can see the glow from these lanterns below illuminate the empty street in front of it, their luminosity announcing who the Lee family is. The party will last a while more. I tiptoe past Number One Madam's room as Ah Poh is asleep on the thin mattress outside her open door. I pad softly past the Eminent Mister Lee's room. The doors to his bed chambers are shut. Laughter trills and glasses clink and a light chatter can be heard as I start to descend the grand stairs heading towards the servant's exit door. My heart is pounding as I can't wait to see Hassan.

'Ah Mei, is that you?' Ah Poh calls out urgently.

I climb back up four steps and walk back towards Number One Madam's chambers. I find Ah Poh seated on her grass mat. A wedge of moonlight emanating from Number One Madam's room shows Ah Poh hugging her knees, curled into a ball.

'Yes, Ah Poh. Are you hungry?'

'No, Ah Mei. I am in pain.'

'Where?'

'In my stomach. I also feel sick, like vomiting.'

I take my candle closer to Ah Poh. Her face is drained in the dim light. The bags under her eyes age her beyond her years. Her forehead is beaded with sweat. The house has electric lights but these are only used when there are guests and never in the sleeping areas except in Eminent Mister Lee's chambers. And under a candlelight, nobody looks good.

I put my right hand on her forehead to feel for a fever. She is clammy to the touch.

'Why don't you lie down and I'll go get you some hot tea?' I help Ah Poh lie down with my free hand, and that is when I see a puddle of blood pooled by Ah Poh's feet.

'Have you bled down there before, Ah Poh?'

Ah Poh is not much younger than me, maybe by a couple of years. She is bleeding very badly. There's too much blood for a monthly bleed, surely.

'Yes, Ah Mei ... but not like this before ... am I dying?'

There is terror in her voice and she chokes back tears.

I can't leave her lying here losing blood. And most importantly, Number One Madam can't find her like this.

'Ah Poh, how long have you been bleeding?'

'I don't know, Ah Mei ... It started this afternoon ... but it's been a while since I bled.'

Then, I remember seeing her awkward entry into the Guest Hall to serve the guests.

'When did the pain start?'

'Am I dying, Ah Mei?'

'I don't know, Ah Poh. I don't want you to die either. That's why you need to tell me when did the pain start?'

'In the afternoon ... just before the dinner party. It's getting worse, Ah Mei. First, it was a dull ache and now I feel like my insides are being pulled out, like my intestines are spilling out.' Ah Poh is out of breath.

That can't be good. Since I started my first bleeding, I've never felt the kind of pain that Ah Poh is describing now. And my bleeds come every month.

It's been a while since I bled.

I need to ask Ah Wan Jie if this is normal.

'Does Number One Madam know that you're not well?'

'I don't dare tell Madam. She will beat me.' Her breathing is feathery.

'Beat you? Why?'

'She beats me for everything.' She whispers and convulses as another wave of pain hits her.

I never knew this. But then again, I don't talk very much to Ah Poh.

I am torn between helping Ah Poh and rushing out to meet Hassan. I only have a short time before Ah Wan Jie needs my help clearing things and washing up.

I help Ah Poh to her feet. Her pants are soaked through and so is the grass mat that she was sleeping on. She leans on me, stumbling to find her balance.

'Let's get you to the outhouse, wash you up.'

The floor boards creak at our weight as we tiptoe away from her sleeping area.

The area around my collarbones starts to heat up. My jade Guanyin feels hot against my neck. I whisper a quick prayer.

The outhouse is a way away from the main house. It is lit by a yellow bulb that comes to life with the pull of a string. An animal scurries past behind us causing me to look back. I see that Ah Poh has left a trail of blood. I help her into the outhouse by lifting her right leg over the raised threshold and she follows dragging her left. She moans, her body twitching in pain next to me. With Ah Poh inside, the outhouse feels like a broom cupboard. I strip Ah Poh's pants off her. Zig-zagging across her upper thighs are horrifying cuts as if someone, some animal, had clawed her. The marks are weepy and the red rivulets trailing down from between her legs join the rivers of gashes on the inside of her thighs. I recoil in shock.

'Ah Poh! What happened?'

Ah Poh howls into the night like an injured dog. She is uncontrollable. Nothing can console her.

As I hold her shaking body, a shadow skirts past and disappears into the surrounding dimness of the outhouse. A sensation, sharp like needles, pricks the air. It fills the shack and seeps into me, and I begin to shake with wrath. My jade Guanyin sears into my flesh and I hear that voice in my head again.

Do something. Stop the outrage. Don't let them get away with it.

Chapter 22

'Mei, go and get the remedy that Ah Poh needs,' Ah Wan Jie says, handing me a piece of paper, 'take Number One Madam's rickshaw.'

The rickshaw stops me outside a shophouse bearing a sign that says Yew Tong Sing Traditional Medicine Shop. An aniseedy tang envelops me as soon as I enter this family-run apothecary. This scent mingles with the herbal and earthy smells of wood, bark and plants. A glass-topped cabinet counter lines one wall of the shop and two men are standing behind it. I spy an array of medicines: a jar of the human-like ginseng root soaking in liquid displayed on the cabinet; on glass shelves locked within the cabinet are medicines in the form of sun-dried lizards, petrified bats, and a wooden box of scallop-shaped pangolin scales. Recently, Ah Wan Jie has been drinking a medicinal soup made up of boiled scrapings of these scales for her arthritis. I have seen her grating a scale once with the coconut grater.

Behind the two men is a wall panelled by square-shaped drawers, each drawer has a gold knob sitting above a red label filled with squiggly black lines that resemble Chinese words. One man is weighing some herbs with a hand-held balance. With his other hand, he places and removes counter-weights until the weighing instrument becomes level. He is serving a nyonya who has her mui tsai standing by her. The mui tsai is holding a basket filled to the brim with vegetables and packages wrapped in paper. Apart from this pair, the shop is quiet. I hear the man holding the weighing scale speaking in Hakka to the other man behind the counter. They seem to be consulting with each other regarding a certain remedy. I don't understand everything, but Hakka has similar inflections to Cantonese which I do understand. Their conversation done, the man turns to the nyonya and starts to say something to her in Fukien. I don't pay attention because I am mindful that I need to get Ah Poh her medicine. I approach the other man with my note.

'Something to rebuild the body and replenish blood loss.' The physician, *sinseh*, reads the note out loud.

'Does Nyonya Lee know how much blood was lost?' He asks, peering at me from behind round metal-rimmed glasses. He is wearing a man's Chinese shirt and I notice that the buttons are expertly sewn.

'I don't know.'

'Do you know?'

'A lot.' I say from memory, though what may seem a lot to me would perhaps not be a lot to the sinseh.

'Is it for a woman or man? The nyonya hasn't specified.'

'A girl. Twelve maybe fourteen years old.'

'A mui tsai?' the sinseh's eyebrows raise as he probes for more information.

'Yes, sinseh, a mui tsai. She is weak.' I puzzle at how he knows this.

'Where is she bleeding from and how long?'

'From inside.' I blush at the intrusion of his question. 'Two days.' But I don't mention the scratches.

'Red blood or brown blood?'

'Red blood.'

'Strong flow or weak flow?'

'Strong, sinseh! The blood flows out of her like water from a pump.'

The sinseh nods his head and turns around to face his wall of medicines, opens a drawer here and another there, picking out the herbs for the cure that Number One Madam has ordered.

'Boil this whole packet of herbs for three hours. When the water darkens, let it cool and feed the girl with it until colour comes back to her face.'

I take the packet and pay him his fee.

'You should've come to me earlier. She has probably lost a lot of blood,' the sinseh says shaking his head.

Chapter 23

I throw the herbs that Ah Mei has returned with into the clay pot used only for boiling medicines. I measure out four bowls of water. There are only enough herbs to boil Ah Poh one pot of medicinal broth, which gives two bowls of remedy.

Since finding out about Ah Poh, Number One Madam has asked that I keep her downstairs in the servants' quarters with me. Ah Mei has given up her bed for Ah Poh and is now sleeping on the floor on a thin grass mat.

This is what I resent—having to take care of the mui tsai. I am feeding Ah Poh her bitter soup when Master Lee storms into the room. In shock, I drop the crockery bowl and the soup spills all over the floor. Blast! I will have to send Ah Mei for another packet of herbs. This has already taken me hours to boil.

'Tell me what happened, Ah Poh?'

His voice is laced with anger. Ah Poh shrinks into the corner of her bed and starts to cry.

'No, no, don't cry. Tell me what had happened to you,' he asks, gentler this time.

'Master Lee,' I say mustering authority in my voice, 'poor Ah Poh is in shock. She won't be able to make sense of what had happened to her.'

'Ah Wan Jie, you're in charge of all the mui tsai, so you must know something.'

I take a deep breath, gather my thoughts. What I have to say is important. But I must also abide by an unspoken rule amongst us servants.

'Ah Poh is bleeding, that's all …'

'How badly? Ah Mei said it was quite bad.'

'Ah Mei?'

Since when did the master of the Lee household listen to a lowly servant girl? Anger rises to my throat. I am reminded that I was right all along about this waif of a girl. She needs to be reined in.

My voice disguises my true feelings. Master Lee mustn't know how I feel.

'Ah Mei, did you say Master Lee?'

'Yes. Ah Mei.' His reply is equally guarded.

'Then Ah Mei must really care about this mui tsai.'

'Look Ah Wan Jie, I am investigating something very important for the Court of Malaya.'

I nod my head. The law that he has no doubt learned to do.

'I am talking to people—my parents, the Chinese merchants and mui tsai.'

This is the most absurd thing I have ever heard since my working days started in the Lee household. Talking to people. Talking to mui tsai. No good master of any distinguished family speaks to their servants apart from ordering them.

'I want to know how Ah Poh came to be bleeding so much.'

At this point, Ah Poh whimpers. And I turn facing her. She has pulled her coverlet under her chin and is shaking her head slowly. Her eyes, round and watery, bore into mine, imploring.

I wonder what has Ah Poh's bleeding to do with the Court of Malaya.

'Master Lee, as you can see Ah Poh is sick. Nothing more than woman trouble, Master Lee. Nothing for a man like you to worry about.'

Master Lee looks at me and nods his head. I was afraid that he would want to take a look at Ah Poh. That would be bad. Embarrassing. I would have to find excuses to hide the fact.

'Well, as long as there is no abuse in the Lee house, I am good. I know that I still need to persuade Ah Pa to let the mui tsai go free. An Ordinance has been passed and it is now illegal to keep mui tsai without registering them.'

Let the mui tsai go free? Where would they go? How will they survive? What law would leave these vulnerable girls so unprotected?

Of course I don't ask these questions out loud.

'Abuse?'

Abuse means that the mui tsai are not treated well, he explains. Like they're not being fed well, always beaten or being taken advantage of. He doesn't explain exactly what he meant by being taken advantage of.

Ah Poh's mewling tells me she knows. My heart sinks to the lowest of depths.

To distract the good master, I lead him out of the bedroom.

'Do not worry, Master Lee. The Lee house treats us well.'

As Master Lee walks back to his world, mine is immediately filled with a familiar and profound dread.

This time, I mustn't let another mui tsai die.

Chapter 24

The Lee house, March 1932

Ah Poh's life force is strong. She is still bleeding but it is not as bad as it was on the first day. It's been nearly a month since her big bleed. Although her breaths are still weak, they are no longer fragile like a dying rabbit's. But she still needs medication.

I have been going to the sinseh so many times now that when he sees me, he knows what remedies to pack, though he asks the same list of questions each time. Today's visit took me by surprise.

'She is still bleeding, sinseh,' I say, 'but lesser than the first time I found her and lesser than the last rounds of medication. I need the same prescription for her, please.'

'What colour is the bleeding? It is bright red or dark red?'

'It looks darker to me.'

'Strong flow or weak flow?'

'Weaker now. The blood seems clumpy and her pain is less.'

'I will put together a stronger mix of herbs. I suspect that she was quit far in and had lost a foetus, and the blood flow is now old blood—clumpy, you said. She is on the mend but she will need more herbal potions and a different type of remedy to bring her health up.'

I let the sinseh's words sink in.

She had lost a foetus.

I left the pharmacy in a daze. The only time I've heard the word foetus was not long after Huat was born and Ma was very sick and had bled a lot like Ah Poh. Surely, Ah Wan Jie must suspect the same thing as the sinseh. She has more experience with women's bodily flows than me. I will ask her.

* * *

I am pounding up some garlic and shallots for the *babi pongteh* that Ah Wan Jie will be cooking later. Her arthritic hands are giving her problems again. As I work, Ah Wan Jie sits on a stool, feet wide apart, the legs of her samfoo pants flapping in the slight mid-morning breeze wafting through the kitchen. She is pouring herself a cup of tea. I wonder what the tea leaves are going to tell me. I won't know until I wash her cup later.

She sips her hot tea and fixes her eyes on me. She is watching me, ready to instruct me to pound harder or softer or not to roll the mortar too much. The rhythmic thudding of the pestle against the stone mortar is soothing, calming, and I formulate the question I intend to ask Ah Wan Jie. It has taken me a couple of days to bring it up. I decide that I will just be direct about it because I don't know any other way to ask this question mired in taboo.

'Ah Wan Jie … the sinseh said … Ah Lian's blood loss … her blood loss … it was cos … cos of … was a foetus.' My words match the pounding rhythm as I continue mincing the garlic and shallots in the pestle and mortar. A pulp is forming and I must stop before it becomes too watery.

'Ah Mei … this is not something that anyone can find out, you hear?'

Ah Wan Jie's voice is urgent, trembling. I sense fear.

'How can Ah Poh lose a foetus, Ah Wan Jie?' I turn to look at her, resting the mortar on the side table where a tray of spices sits.

'You listen to me, Ah Mei … I do not want another life on my hands.'

I am confused by Ah Wan Jie's response. She didn't answer my question but it seems that my asking has perturbed her.

Her words hang in my mind like Number One Madam's batik sarongs drying on the bamboo pole. *I don't want another life on my hands* flap about in my head as I process the meaning of Ah Wan Jie's words.

My thoughts take me back to the day when Percy Lee changed the sleeping arrangements. On Percy Lee's insistence, I have now moved into Ah Yoke's room. Percy Lee will not have me sleeping on the floor. When Ah Wan Jie heard Percy Lee's instructions, her face turned pale. She started to mutter a prayer to Guanyin for protection.

'Ah Wan Jie, I can stay with Ah Poh, if you want. You sleep with Ah Yoke,' I offered a solution, seeing that she was concerned about the new arrangements.

'No, no, I would rather stay in my own room, even if it's with a sick girl.'

Ah Wan Jie made like she's about to tell me something more but then stopped.

'Ah Wan Jie, what is it?'

'Ah Lian used to sleep in Ah Yoke's room as you know. And the arrangement did not bode well for her. You stay alert, you hear?'

'Ah Wan Jie, you say something but also tell me nothing at all. What happened to Ah Lian?'

'There is nothing to tell, Ah Mei. Ah Lian was unfortunate. She made a mistake. I'm sure you're wiser than her.'

The pulped shallots in the mortar start to sting my eyes. I blink away the tears, wishing Ah Wan Jie would just answer my question. I want to know what happened to Ah Lian and if Ah Poh had really lost a baby, and how did she even have a baby. And why is Ah Wan Jie so afraid it's her fault—whose life is she talking about? But, instead of saying more, Ah Wan Jie gets up and tosses the remainder of her tea into the plant pot next to her. Now, I will never know what the tea leaves say, if Ah Wan Jie was lying to me or skirting the truth. I am left with a knot of frustration in my stomach.

Then, I hear that voice again.

Don't let them get away with it.

'Who is them, get away with what?' I hiss back a response.

'What … what are you saying, Ah Mei?' Ah Wan Jie's voice is laced with irritation, 'I don't have time for your silly nonsensical mumblings now, you hear? Let's just focus on getting Ah Poh better,' she continues after a short pause, her voice determined. And then, she adds, 'You're as responsible for Ah Poh as much as I am, Ah Mei. She came to you for help, like Ah Lian had come to me. We are in this together. You must help Ah Poh.'

At that point, I excuse myself to check on Ah Poh's herbal concoction that Ah Wan Jie had asked me to boil. The air in the kitchen smells of medicine and moisture. Rain is coming. I'm not sure why I am as responsible as Ah Wan Jie but since we are in this together, I better make sure that Ah Poh gets her medicine in time. I scoop some herbal potion into a bowl for Ah Poh's next feed. I smell its potent bitterness. Every spoonful pulls her closer back to this world.

Chapter 25

The afternoon downpour has now subsided. It's just as well or I won't be able to see Hassan at all. Hassan is already there when I step out in the alley from the back door. The rain has left behind some puddles in the alleyway. Other than a couple of drips from the gutter above us, we won't get wet out here. I take my place next to Hassan, sitting on our usual stone slab. He's lined it with old newspapers to keep our bottoms dry. I start recounting the day's events to Hassan. He listens to me intently to the end without interruption.

'Ah Wan Jie did not make any sense this morning, Hassan. And she refused to answer my question.'

'Well, the important thing is that Ah Poh is better. I'm relieved to know this,' he says, his voice warm and sincere, 'for a young girl like her to experience this … it must be very traumatic.' He continues after a short pause.

I nod in agreement.

'I don't know why Kakak Wan is making you responsible for Ah Poh either … seems like she wants you to share her burden.'

I can't explain why I know this, but there is something beneath Hassan's voice that tells me there's more going on in his mind than relief. I wait a while before telling him about the shadow at the outhouse.

'Hassan, that night in the outhouse when I was with Ah Poh ... I saw something ... felt something ... a strong energy.'

I feel Hassan's hand tighten around mine. I feel his love strong and secure.

'I felt a strong feeling of ... of ... anger, Hassan ... it was so strong that it scared me.'

'Mei, I am angry too, at the injustice of it all ... at how Ah Poh nearly lost her life ... that she was violated in such a way ... that since Ah Lian's death, nothing has stopped.'

'Hassan, what do you ... what do you know about Ah Lian?'

'Mei, it's not my story to tell as I'd said ... I shouldn't have brought her name up ...'

Hassan pauses before saying, '... all you need to know is that Ah Lian wasn't as lucky as Ah Poh ... and I am sure there are many Ah Lians in this city.'

How could Ah Poh's fate be considered lucky, I thought. I know that Ah Lian lost her life ... but Ah Poh lost another life. I was about to voice this when Hassan continues —

'... that is why, Mei, we must set ourselves free—' Hassan was going to say more when the sky above darkens with a moving blanket of black clouds. A tittering of magpies flies overhead. They move like a wave above us and in their dance, a bridge forms. And as quickly as the bridge was built, the arc of black disperses and the magpies fly one group in one direction and another in the opposite, and the sky is a burnt orange again, the sun ready to set.

A sweet melody echoes in the air. And then, just as soon as the birds start to sing, their song fades quickly into the dusky environment disappearing with the bridge of magpies. The alley is suddenly so quiet that the only sound I can hear is the beating of my heart.

The silence is broken by Hassan.

'Whoa, what was that, Mei?' Hassan says, standing up and cupping his eyes to catch another glimpse of the birds.

I stand up too and we both search the sky. A sensation of relief flows through me, giving way to a sense of freedom, something I have not felt before. I feel light. I feel that I can take flight. I feel free like the magpies in the sky.

'I feel so free, Mei,' Hassan says as if reading my thoughts. He turns around and gives me the tightest hug. Hassan lifts me off my feet and spins me round. We are both laughing.

Chapter 26

Hassan and I sit back down on the concrete slab covering the drain below. Leaning against the exit door of the kitchen, we are both lost in our thoughts. I am grateful for these moments because every minute I get to spend with Hassan is a victory against the cruel hands of Fate.

I don't like the alleyway much. The rubbish in the drain chokes me with acrid smells of decay. The night soil buckets along the walls stink of sulphur and excrement. I have learnt to douse my hanky with some nutmeg oil and when the smells get bad, I breathe into my hanky and let the scent of nutmeg quell the nausea.

A rat, its whiskers twitching menacingly, scurries across the alley and disappears into the drain opposite. As bad as it is, this is the only place that Hassan and I can meet without being caught. On some evenings, when he can, he brings a Roti John sandwich to share. He will always recite one of Tagore's poems by heart. I listen intently, swimming in an ocean of beautiful words, lost in Hassan's world.

'The Roti John Poetry Club,' Hassan said one evening. 'The two of us are our own little poetry club.' My heart is squeezed with myriad emotions like all the words that Tagore has used to describe love and longing.

Tonight a miracle has occurred.

'This is a phenomenon, Mei,' Hassan says, 'the birds flying like this in silent formation. I have never seen something like this before.'

'They are magpies, Hassan … magical birds. Their song—so beautiful, isn't it?'

The words tumble out of me, yet I do not know how I have this knowledge. I just know these birds are magpies.

'Yes, they sing so beautifully. And they're powerful too … kinda like in the story you told me of the Cowherd and the Weaver Girl.' He smiles at me and gives me another tight hug. I detect a faint scent of earthy turmeric.

Hassan relaxes and lets out a long, contented sigh. I relax too, letting go of thoughts of Ah Lian for now. Seeing the magpies has opened a window to another world for both Hassan and me. I feel strong, good and full of hope.

'Mei, the other day, a woman, I've not seen her before, came to the shop.' There is hope in his voice.

'She's from India, like me. But she's different. Her religion is known as Bahá'í.' The sliver of hope peeking through Hassan's voice makes me hopeful too.

'Did she come to tell you about her faith?'

'No, no! She was handing out pamphlets, Mei.'

'Pamphlets? Like newspapers?'

'Not really … pamphlets are like pieces of paper with information …'

Hassan stops, deep in thought.

'She's giving a talk in Hock Chew Park on Pickering Street and I think we should go listen to her.' He looks at me. The glow in his eyes match the shine of his smile.

'What information was on the paper?'

'The title of the pamphlet said *Fighting for Our Freedom*. It's in two days. In the afternoon, she said.'

I nod, digesting the information he's sharing.

'We must go Mei, I have a good feeling about it. I think what she has to say is important.'

I desperately want to go but how can I slip out in the afternoon when it's the busiest time of the day? Number One Madam and the little wives would be having their afternoon naps and after they would likely entertain some visitors. And whilst they're having their siesta, I have to get on with the chores. In three days, Eminent Mister Lee will be expecting some important guests, Ah Wan Jie has already informed me. There are tea time snacks to prepare. She is making those five spiced rolls again as Percy Lee will be present to meet these important guests. And I must help her with the *pulut inti*, the glutinous rice pouches with sweet coconut. So much preparation for an event taking place in three days is the norm in the Lee household because Eminent Mister Lee needs to look good, as Ah Wan Jie keeps reminding me. And that's just preparing the food because the food and the service must be immaculate. And, since Ah Poh is still too weak to serve, I have been tasked to do that. I have never served important guests before and I am anxious just thinking about it. What if I drop the tray of food? Worse, spill tea all over Eminent Mister Lee?

'I can't, Hassan, you know I can't … Number One Madam will need my help as Ah Poh is still weak. And Ah Wan Jie also needs me to help her with the pulut inti … And Ah Yoke, what do I do with her?'

Hassan remains quiet but I can feel his brain firing up with ideas.

'Don't worry, my moon goddess and the polar star of my life. I have a plan.'

His words make me giggle. Hassan always has a way to disentangle the knot in my stomach and ease my fears.

'I will pretend to deliver something to the Lee house. With all that food that needs preparing, Ah Wan Jie will need stuff. You try to steal out—tell Ah Wan Jie you're going to buy something for her, say glutinous rice for the pulut inti. She will need some of that, I'm guessing. Tell her she's missing glutinous rice. Oh, and tell her that she'll also need some rice. It's been a week and more since she's ordered the Thai rice that Number One Madam likes.'

He rattles off, his voice full of conviction that his plan will work. I am infected with a strong sense of faith too.

Chapter 27

'Ah Wan Jie, we need more rice.'

I force myself to sound convinced that we are in short supply of rice. Then I offer to go buy rice like in Hassan's plan.

'What? *Yum Gong*, oh my goodness, really?' Ah Wan Jie mutters a string of Cantonese words.

She checks the rice bin and sure enough, Hassan is right, we need more Thai rice.

'Ah Wan Jie, we also need some glutinous rice. Remember the pulut inti? And coconut?'

I am getting good at this game.

'Thank goodness, I have you, Ah Mei. What would I do without your sharp eye and memory? Go, go to Encik Abdullah's this afternoon … I will need—'

Ah Wan Jie rattles off her shopping list. I am beaming from ear to ear.

'What you smiling about?'

And my smile drops.

'Nothing … nothing, Ah Wan Jie … just listening to your orders and making a mental list of them myself.'

'Ok, we will be busy, girl, so nothing to smile about. It's all work, you hear?'

I nod.

When the household is having their siesta, I leave for Encik Abdullah's with my heart in my throat. In a stroke of good luck, Ah Wan Jie has let me leave Ah Yoke with her.

I walk briskly all the way to Encik Abdullah's. Hassan is waiting for me in the back alley a little distance away from his uncle's shop. We walk towards town, where Hock Chew Park is. It's not far from the kuih-kuih shop where Percy Lee took Ah Yoke and me to buy *ang ku kuih*, his father's favourite dessert.

Along the way, I spy a European-looking building with a long and tall house attached to the main one. Hassan explains that this is a convent. The tall house is where the bells are kept, he says. This explains the chiming sounds I am hearing. The bells pealing offers a soothing balm to what Hassan has to say about this place.

Baby girls, especially those born in the Year of the Tiger, are left there at the doorstep to be picked up by the nuns living in this convent. They take care of these unwanted girls and send them to good homes. Tiger girls, unwanted and left to die or given away, is not news to me because Ah Mah had many stories of abandoned Tiger girls, yet, I marvel at Hassan's worldly knowledge. I don't know how he knows these things but I think that it must be the ability to read that makes him so intelligent.

I don't know much about European convents but I am relieved that Tiger girl babies have somewhere to go. I can imagine the convent being like the Po Leung Kuk, a half-way house, set up to take in young women who have run away from brothels and little girls who nobody wants. Ah Ping Yee volunteers there and she often tells Ah Wan Jie about the girls and how the home prepares young girls for marriage, saving them from disgrace. Many have been saved from the brothels because of the Po Leung Kuk. As for the babies left at this half-way home, they're taken care of by the older girls and women and when the time is right, adopted out to good families. Yet, some still fall through the net. I shudder as I remember Ah Wan Jie's story of the young mui tsai who had a sloughing skin disease that Number One Madam sold off to a prostitution den.

'How do you know about the convent, Hassan, and what they do?'

'Pak Abdullah uses old newspapers that he buys from the rag-and-bone man to wrap things up with,' Hassan says, 'and when he's not looking, I read the news this way.'

The rag-and-bone man is what Ah Wan Jie calls the *karang guni ah-sook*, the old uncle who comes and buys the newspapers and old things that the Lee household throws out. I often hear Ah Wan Jie greet this man in Cantonese, *ah-sook, ah-sook*, as if he is her uncle, and they banter as she haggles for more money and he tries to pay her less for the rubbish she's selling. Now, I know who buys up all these old news-worthy papers for reuse.

'... and the mui tsai gossip as well. That's how I know where unwanted baby girls go.'

I let out a deep sigh. That unwanted girl could've been me, if I were born a Tiger.

* * *

The park is already crowded when we arrive. We mustn't draw attention to ourselves. Hassan suggests that we should make ourselves scarce like he is reading my thoughts. I don't see other mui tsai there. This doesn't surprise me. There are Malay and Indian women in the crowd. Men like Eminent Mister Lee amongst them. I spot a few Chinese women in their samfoo and a couple in elegant *cheongsams*, but no nyonya, like Number One Madam. Soon, a group of European women arrive, carrying placards.

The murmurs in the park quieten into silence as the woman from India starts to speak. She stands on a stage and her voice is loud and clear. Then I see a familiar woman. She has golden hair. It is Mrs Smith and she is in front of the stage with her husband and some other ang moh ladies from the church.

The Indian lady is called Shirin Fozdar. She introduces herself and starts to tell the crowd that she believes in equality and liberty. That for the world to be a better place, people need to be kind, compassionate and accepting of other people. That love is the only cure for the cruelty and violence that is happening in the world we live in.

As she speaks, some people in the crowd cheer. Her energy is very infectious. Her passion audible through the microphone that carries her voice to everyone.

Then I hear the word 'mui tsai' together with 'vulnerable' mixed with words like 'violation of human rights' and 'abuse', and these are peppered by words such as law and ordinance and British government. Her speech is in English and someone translates her sentences into Malay as soon as she finishes one, and another person adds meaning in Fukien as soon as the Malay words leave their speaker's lips. In this three-way passing of words, I manage to understand that an important thing is happening and soon mui tsai like me would be free.

Hassan hears it too. He hugs me close to him.

Freedom is coming soon.

His breath against my ear as he whispers these words sends an electric sizzle along my spine.

Chapter 28

As soon as Mrs Shirin Fozdar finishes her speech, the crowd starts to disperse. Many are rushing off because of a threatening thunder cloud in the distance and the beginning of a drizzle. When the crowd thins, Hassan takes my hand and we leave our hiding place behind the huge girth of a flame-of-the-forest tree. I am too elated to remember that such public display of affection as Hassan holding my hand is frowned upon.

A string of whistles follow us. They are from a bunch of coolies on a break from their jobs at the river not far from the park.

'Aye, don't anyhow touch the girl, *ampuneh*!'

Hassan whips his head to face the direction of those stinging words.

Keh-leng. Smelly Indian. Snake.

'Let's ignore them, Mei.' I feel his grip tighten and we walk away from the slurs. 'They're spoiling for a fight, tired of their hard work and low pay. I suspect also high from opium.'

Hassan lets go of my hand at the same time as someone with a leer steps in front of me. His breath stinks of rotting teeth laced with a burnt sweetness that I've only ever smelled on Ah Pa on the rare occasions he came home. The leering face pushes Hassan and he tumbles backwards and falls on his haunches. Horrid laughter and more hurtful words follow. Then, the face places two open palms on my chest, he squeezes my breasts before pushing me, making me fall down, and saying things in Fukien that make me blush.

I am not that kind of girl. I am not a wanton wench. I am not a prostitute.

Incensed, I scramble to my feet, find my balance and steady myself to push the leering face if he pushes me again. Next to me, Hassan tries to get up, but the coolie kicks him hard and this time, Hassan falls flat on his back. The coolie steps towards me. I step back, feet apart, ready to fight back. Behind the coolie is the man with the cloudy eyes.

'Go away,' I say vehemently to the apparition. The leering face laughs and the ghost turns his back and ambles away, disappearing behind the tree. The coolie is about to push me again when Hassan's voice distracts him.

'Stop it, Ah-beng kia!' Hassan shouts, stumbling to get up, 'leave the girl alone.'

Hassan shouldn't have used this Fukien term, *kia*, calling him a boy, infantilizing the coolie, who is a man. He would surely be even more furious now.

Hassan is on his feet, standing slightly in front of me, protecting me from the angry Chinese man. I can see the coolie's nostrils flaring and his leer more sour than before. There is a deadly fury in his eyes. What is he going to do now? Will he push Hassan again? Touch me again? My train of thought is followed by an echoing laughter. The laughter metamorphoses into a tussle and Hassan is on top of the Chinese coolie, the two of them scrabbling on the grass. Punches ensue. I scream. Blood pours out of the coolie's nose.

'Break it up, the pair of you!'

An authoritative voice accompanies a pair of hands breaking up the coolie and Hassan. It's a voice I know. Hassan rolls away from the coolie's grasp. Then, a fisted hand flies across the air landing on the middle of the leering face hitting him square on the bridge of his nose. More blood flows. The coolie runs off clutching his broken nose, his gang of hooligans following.

The familiar voice doesn't give chase. Instead he offers a hand to Hassan and helps him off the grassy turf.

Chapter 29

The familiar voice is Percy Lee.

'What are you doing here, Mei?' Percy Lee asks genuinely curious, 'does Mother know?'

I shake my head in shame.

'No matter, she doesn't need to know.'

Percy Lee sounds concerned yet there is understanding in his voice.

Hassan hangs back, not knowing what to do.

'Master Lee, I am here with my friend Hassan Mohamed. Came to listen to Mrs Fozdar.'

'Yes, what she had to say was important ... *is* important. Did you understand most of her message, Mei?'

I nod and look Percy Lee in the eye. His smile reaches his dark brown eyes. It is warm, encouraging, kind.

Hassan steps forward and proffers a hand inviting a handshake. Percy Lee returns the gesture.

'Hello, Hassan!'

'Master Lee.'

'Call me Percy. I guess we're here for the same reasons, aren't we?'

'Yes, to hear what Mrs Fozdar has to say and to understand the situation,' I reply and Hassan nods in agreement. I am surprised at my audacity but speaking up brings with it a newfound liberty.

'It's all good news, Mei,' Percy Lee says, affirming Mrs Fozdar's message, 'this means that you and all the mui tsai would be legal as soon as Ah Pa registers your status. You'll be paid and you can leave if you're unhappy with your employer and find new work. In short, you'll be protected by the Mui-Tsai Ordinance, which became a law in January this year.'

Freedom.

Hassan whispers this word. Percy Lee states it out loud.

Percy Lee, Hassan and I walk back to the Lee household refreshed and full of hope.

Chapter 30

Ah Yoke peeks through the latticed divider observing the guests in the Guest Hall arriving one by one. They are all men. I am surprised to see a European man as this is the first time I've seen one so close and one so tall as well.

Percy Lee shakes the hands of the tall European man and greets him as Mister Pickering. To my Fukien ears, this British name sounds more like Pi-keh-leng, the last character, the sound meaning dragon.

'Ah Mei Jie, tall man, look!' Ah Yoke whispers in glee.

I hush her because I don't want to be caught.

The night before, Number One Madam had asked to see me. This was the first time in nearly eight months since my arrival that she has shown any interest in seeing me. It turned out that all she wanted to do was to make sure that I am clean and have a good set of samfoo to wear. Clean, she emphasized sternly, without looking at me. I am to serve the guests, she said. She won't be there as Nyonya women are not permitted to be in business meetings but she will know if I do something wrong. Ah Wan Jie is in charge but she won't be serving since there is a chance that she may cause an accident because of her arthritic hands.

'Do not make me lose face,' Number One Madam said, still without looking at me, 'do not spill or drop any food on Eminent Mister and Master Lee, do you understand?'

Of course I nodded to that instruction.

What about the other guests? Surely, I must also not spill food and drinks on them.

'I will cane you properly if you do.'

I wondered then what Miss Tang Siu Lan would do as Percy Lee's wife. Would being married to a modern man permit her to sit at business meetings like this one? Would it also mean that she would stop mui tsai from being beaten?

Number One Madam treated me like I was a piece of the furniture. Ah Wan Jie often tells me the intimate conversations that she and Number One Madam have. I didn't sense that Number One Madam would be intimate, share her thoughts, with me at last night's meeting. I pushed those thoughts out of my mind and concentrated on the rest of what Number One Madam had to say. They were all instructions to do this and that. I will do my best, of course. Then she said something quite strange and inappropriate I felt.

'If the Eminent Mister Lee takes an interest in your status and welfare, you are to let me know.'

My status. My welfare. Takes interest. Let me know. Number One Madam's words droned in my ears.

Chapter 31

'Ah Yoke stay here until I come get you,' I whisper in her ears, 'don't make a sound, ok?' She nods her head, eyes glued ahead, peeking from behind the latticed divider into the Guest Hall.

Back in the kitchen, I smooth down some creases on my samfoo and make sure that my collar is not loose. I check my appearance using the large silver service platter. My own face staring back is unfamiliar. The only reflection of myself I see are on window panes when I clean them, and I never linger long over how I look. The silver platter shows a worried face, there are frown lines on my forehead. I lift my lips and smile back at myself to smoothen out the lines before I load the platter with the five-spiced rolls, a dish of sambal and another containing a sweetened black sauce, placing the pot of chrysanthemum tea in the middle to balance the weight. Just like how Ah Wan Jie had shown me. I count out the teacups—five—and put them around the teapot, not stacking them. *Don't stack the teacup*, Ah Wan Jie had said, *bad luck*.

Mister Pickering is accompanied by a Chinese man in European clothing, like what Percy Lee is wearing too. And Mr Tang forms the third guest, representing the Chinese Merchants Association. Like Percy Lee and the other Chinese man, Mister Tang is also in a western suit. The only man wearing a Chinese suit is the Eminent Mister Lee. The platter is heavy and I must be careful that I don't trip, breaking the precious porcelain teapot and teacup set. These, Ah Wan Jie had said, were made to order by the late Lee patriarch, Percy Lee's grandfather, and shipped from Jingdezhen in Southern China, where expensive China-ware are made. It is an heirloom, she had said, and used only to serve tea to the most distinguished of guests.

The conversation is quite lively as I enter to serve the teatime snacks, my heart beating hard and fast, the trembling of the teacups on the silver platter echoing my heartbeats. Eminent Mister Lee is encircling a goblet of brandy in his right hand, looking like he's exercising his wrist. The crystal decanter, sitting in the middle of the round dining table, containing this oolong-coloured spirit is sparkling. Mister Pickering is sipping his brandy as I walk into the room. I place the silver platter on the table with a little too much force than expected. Luckily, nobody minded, even though I am wedged in between Eminent Mister Lee and Mister Pickering. I distribute the food and teacups and pour each gentleman a cup of the floral tea, its light-yellow tone in contrast to that of the brandy the men are drinking. Percy Lee is speaking as I place the precious teapot in the middle of the table, next to the crystal decanter, for the men to pour the chrysanthemum tea out themselves when they want. I glance up and see his lips move but I don't understand what Percy Lee is saying.

Then, I feel something creeping up my legs. It starts with a sensation of someone stroking the back of my left thigh followed by a gentle pat on my buttocks and a then a squeeze of my right buttock cheek. I freeze in my place. My eyes dart left and right searching for the owner of this touch. Mister Pickering's elbows are resting on the table, brandy goblet by his right hand. My heart quickens with each squeeze of my buttocks.

'The Ordinance obliges all mui tsai to be registered,' Mr Pickering says in Fukien, 'making them legal entities. The Chinese community has not been proactive about this. The Ordinance was passed two months ago, Baba Lee. Perhaps—'

The squeezes stop. I collect the debris of peanut shells and cigarette packets on the marble-top table and am backing away towards the exit door when I hear Eminent Mister Lee shouting at me to stay put. Startled by the shock of his booming voice, I lower the silver platter. The platter hits my knee caps causing my legs to go weak. Everything on the platter scatters on the floor. I am mortified. I hold the silver platter tight to my chest not daring to take another step.

'Mui tsai means little sister, Mister Pickering, or if you will, little daughters,' Eminent Mister Lee explains, his voice hard and unyielding, 'I have in my household a number of these little girls whom I've adopted, providing their families with a source of income and saving their daughters from a life of disgrace, destitute and deprivation.'

Mr Tang agrees loudly and vehemently.

'Father,' Percy Lee interrupts Eminent Mister Lee, 'it is against the law to keep mui tsai without—'

Eminent Mister Lee coughs, warning his son that he has been out of line. Then, he stands up, turns and grabs my face with one hand, squeezing my cheeks so tightly that my lips pucker, and says, 'See this mui tsai? She is my daughter and I can do what the hell I please with her.'

Percy Lee starts another sentence and before he can say anything more, Eminent Mister Lee storms out of the Guest Hall. The silver platter clatters on the floor and a pressing ache starts at the base of my nape working its way up to my head. Heat is emanating from my jade pendant. I am shaking with anger.

Chapter 32

I am glad that I threw my tea out before Ah Mei could tell me what the leaves say. It is not right for a girl to be able to sense these things. I see her. I see her looking quizzically at me each time she reads my tea leaves. Well, not this time.

Ah Poh lies on the mattress moaning softly as I feed her another bowl of herbal medicine. I wonder when she will get better. This remedy smells a little stronger than the last. The sinseh must have changed the prescription. The blood is thinning but it hasn't stopped flowing.

Number One Madam has not once come to ask after Ah Poh, and it's been more than a month.

The same rules apply.

Her voice reverberates in my mind. I pray that Ah Poh recovers soon. At least I don't have to take care of disposing a baby this time. And if Ah Poh is well again, maybe Number One Madam will not be asking me to apply any of her rules.

I am not happy that the sinseh had divulged so much information to Ah Mei. What is it with this girl that makes everyone want to share their innermost thoughts with her? I need to get to the bottom of things. Did Ah Poh lose a foetus like what the sinseh had said. And how did she get those horrible gashes on her thighs? I have been applying a herbal tincture on them and they're getting better. The deeper gashes will leave marks, I'm sure.

'Ah Poh … tell Ah Wan Jie about those scratches, Ah Poh,' I ask gently as I feed her another spoonful of the black bitter soup.

Ah Poh shakes her head. Her eyes well up again. She chokes on her medicine.

'Okay, okay, if it pains you, you don't have to say anything, but I will not be responsible for your sins, you hear.'

Tears stream silently down Ah Poh's cheeks. I am irritated that she will not confide in me. How can I help her if she stays silent? I know that a mui tsai has no might to stop what their masters do to her. A mui tsai four doors away just became the sixth wife of the master, Mister Lo. Six wives! Men seem to collect wives like they collect furniture. I heard from Ping-chieh that the mui tsai had given birth to the patriarch's son and that was why she was added to his list of wives. At least, they didn't throw her out and take her son away from her. Ah Lian's baby would have been spared if Fate had dealt a fairer hand of cards. Ah Lian could even have been married to the Eminent Mister Lee if she had given him a son instead of a lousy daughter. And I wouldn't have had to steal away in the night to leave the helpless bundle for some *kwailo* nuns to pick up. Ah Lian would still be alive if she had just swallowed her pride not swallow a well full of putrid water. She was hoping that the Eminent Mister Lee would honour her. What a silly girl. Didn't she know that a girl who spreads her legs this easily is never respected?

Mother was right in telling me to not get married. A Chinese woman is never assured that she remains the only wife. And it doesn't matter if the man is wealthy or poor. Of course, the wealthier they are, the more wives they collect, like trophies to line the wall of the Guest Hall. But then look at Father, he's not wealthy, only an ordinary bus conductor and still he had another wife behind Mother's back. How it broke Mother's heart. How it made me so angry to see my mother weep and beat her chest chastising herself for being born a lowly woman. Mother Guanyin, I need your compassion right now.

'Come on now, Ah Poh, finish the last spoon of this potent soup. It will make you better.'

I don't want to have to apply the same rules with you, I say to myself. The Po Leung Kuk wasn't Number One Madam's choice for Ah Lian. It was mine. That was the best I could do. Number One Madam had wanted me to take Ah Lian to a brothel in Chinatown and leave her there. *Yum goong*, good God, what a cruel thing to do. So, I applied the rules my way. Still, I couldn't save Ah Lian.

As Ah Poh opens her mouth wide, I tell myself to remind Ping-chieh that I want to go through the hair-combing ceremony too and take a vow of celibacy. With so much going on in this godforsaken house, I haven't had the time to be proactive. I must act soon. If there are any rules to apply, this one belongs to me. I will keep my body to myself.

'Yes, open your mouth and not your legs, Ah Poh.' I think to myself as I give the last spoonful of her bitter medicine.

I turn to leave and Ah Lian's wretched face glares at me from behind Ah Poh's blazing eyes.

Chapter 33

Seven days have gone by since the day of the meeting. I did not embarrass the Eminent Mister Lee by spilling tea on him, even though I very much wanted to scald him with hot tea. I didn't like the way he had grabbed my face and the way he had touched me. But I don't tell Ah Wan Jie any of this, only that I didn't spill food and drinks on anyone, including the guests. Ah Wan Jie was pleased with my performance and she reported it to Number One Madam.

If the Eminent Mister Lee takes an interest in your status and welfare, you are to let me know.

I lie on my thin cotton mattress pondering on the last words that Number One Madam had said to me. They are cryptic and I am trying to make sense of them. Ah Yoke is asleep as my mind wanders: Why would Eminent Mister Lee take an interest in my status? Well, he has taken a different kind of interest in me, that I know. But what is my status? As far as I know, I am a mui tsai, almost of marriageable age. It is Number One Madam's responsibility to find me a suitable marriage when

I turn eighteen. As I think of this, my heart sinks because Hassan is the only man I want to marry.

We will be free soon.

Hassan's promise brings respite and I am eager to get to the end of the bridge where freedom waits. But who will build that bridge for us?

Ah Yoke lets out wispy sighs of contentment as she continues sleeping. My mind drifts to thoughts of Hassan and other things. Even though Number One Madam does not pay Ah Yoke any attention, busy that she already is with running the house and now Percy Lee's imminent marriage, Ah Yoke is nonetheless a contented and cheerful soul.

I watch Ah Yoke's chest undulate with each breath and remember Huat, who must have grown a little taller by now. What I would give to be with Huat right now. How I miss him so. I want to go back to that world I knew before I discovered the world of Lee Guang Hoe. Before he soiled me with his hands that have never done a day's work. How can he be known as Eminent Mister Lee?

* * *

When we met out in the alley the following night after the meeting, Hassan was so outraged to learn what had happened.

'It wasn't Mister Pickering, Hassan.'

'Of course not. Pickering is the Chinese Protector. His job is to look after vulnerable girls and to make sure that the coolies aren't fighting and rioting,' Hassan blurted, 'and he has done a good job so far.'

'I can't believe it's Eminent Mister Lee, Hassan. How could it be possible?'

Hassan took my hands and put something in them.

'Tie the latch and bolt with this string to lock it from the inside, now that you no longer have the key to Ah Yoke's room,' Hassan instructed me, avoiding my question. I've not seen Hassan this incensed before. And this nervous as well.

'What's the matter, Hassan?' I sensed that he had more to say. 'Ah Yoke is fine, I wake up instantly when she starts sleep walking. And tonight, I'd locked her door with a hairpin. It's strange that the key is gone.'

'It's not for Ah Yoke, my moon goddess.' Hassan said as his right arm on my shoulder pulled me closer to him. 'But good thinking with the hairpin. Keep locking the door with it.' Then, he reached his left arm over to give me a hug.

I found myself catching my breath as Hassan squeezed out every emotion welling up in me. A scrawny cat scampered by our feet. It was almost morning. Hassan and I had been chatting all night and soon we must part and go back to our daily grind.

'Don't forget—lock the door with the hairpin and secure it tight with the string tonight, Mei. You're my moon and star, and I will protect you.'

I slunk back into the Lee kitchen while it was still empty. A cockerel signalled the start of a new day as I sneaked back upstairs to Ah Yoke's room. There was still enough time left for a little rest. I twirled the raffia string around my finger as I made plans to bolt the door with it that night.

* * *

The day has slipped through my fingers like the rice grains I rinse daily for cooking. I eat my dinner in silence, exhausted from the lack of sleep and anxious about the night ahead. I can feel the piece of raffia against my left thigh through my trouser pocket, reminding me of what I need to do later.

Ah Yoke is all washed and ready for bed. As soon as I close the door to her room, I lock it with my hairpin and tie the raffia string around the bolt, just as Hassan had asked me to do. Yet I can't stop my heart from pounding against my ribcage. Ah Yoke is sitting at the edge of her bed with her head against my chest as I run a comb through her hair. I feel my body going through the motions of our night-time routine. I am physically present, but my mind is some place else.

Why would the Eminent Mister Lee take an interest in me? Why would Number One Madam even think he would? And the way he had touched me, does that mean he is interested in me? Why?

'Ouch, don't pull so hard!' Ah Yoke's yelp brings me back. She lifts her head and looks at me, her eyes full of confusion. I look at her comb in my right hand and see a bunch of Ah Yoke's black hair bunched up in between its teeth.

'Sorry, Ah Yoke, I didn't mean to yank so hard—we're done now! It's time you go to sleep.'

She rubs her sore head as she climbs into her bed. She tosses and turns to find her sweet spot, curls into a ball, hugging her bedtime rag. I am used to this now. I know that I must wait for Ah Yoke to settle down before I can pull a thin sheet over her.

'Night, night, Ah Yoke!'

'Night, Mei-jie.' She mumbles before putting her right thumb into her mouth. Her thumb fills the hole in the roof of her mouth and because of her condition, the sound of her sucking her thumb is fairly loud. I am used to this noise now, and find comfort in it, somehow. I know that Ah Yoke is asleep when the sucking sound stops. It never takes Ah Yoke long to fall asleep.

A lizard clicks as I make my way to my corner of the room. The room is all quiet, except for the sound of Ah Yoke's breathing. From my mattress, I watch a crack of moonlight dance on the wooden floor. Ah Yoke's fluttery breaths have become soft snores. I glance over at her and see her right arm hanging over the edge of the bed. She is no longer sucking her thumb. Ah Yoke is secure in a deep sleep. But sleep doesn't come for me, tired as I am. I no longer feel safe in the house that has become my home. My heart beats hard and fast, and my underarms are wet with fear even though I have fastened the door with Hassan's raffia string. I can't stop wondering why Eminent Mr Lee would stroke the backs of my thighs the way he did. Did his touch have something to do with what Number One Madam had said? I am still thinking about Number One Madam's cryptic message and Eminent Mister Lee's intentions when the door to Ah Yoke's room starts to rattle. In the dim light, I can see the door shaking. My heart is now in my mouth.

The rattling becomes more forceful. Whoever it is wants very badly to come into Ah Yoke's room. My thoughts go to what Hassan did: *Why did Hassan not answer my question and give me a piece of string instead? Is this why?* The door is shaking even harder now from the force trying to pry it open. The raffia string may come loose soon, I think. I cower in my corner of the room watching the door, praying to Guanyin goddess asking her to protect me from the monster on the other side. My jade pendant gets hotter and hotter with each muttered prayer.

I am incensed by the persistent rattling, also very confused and frightened. My brain is throbbing as red spots like small glass beads jump about in my mind's eye. The beads dance around and start to be joined by a thread winding its way through the servants' quarters, where Ah Poh is convalescing, wrapping itself around Ah Wan Jie, moving along the corridor up the stairwell to wrap itself around Number One Madam, finding its way to Ah Yoke's room and wrapping itself around me. I become cocooned by the thread as it continues to unspool, leaving my head uncovered. I feel constricted. I cannot breathe.

Don't let him get away with it.

The voice in my head shouts. My nape throbs. Something is tugging at my mole. A raw anger escalates along with the rattling.

'Go away,' I shout with a might so great that the rattling stops. I do not recognize the sound of my voice. I feel a magnetic charge ripple through me, causing my joints to ache. But I also feel drained and extremely fatigued. Yet my body is sizzling with a force I cannot control. The cocoon disintegrates and I suck deeply, breathing again. I feel myself being lifted off the ground. My feet are now hanging slightly above the floor boards. My legs dangle loose and free and I levitate towards the bedroom door. Lifting my hands, I place both palms on the door frame. My head bends towards the door as if it was being pulled by a string attached to my crown, and I rest my forehead on the door. I am giddy with something unspeakable. I feel my face contorting and twisting with rage. My body is shaking and I can't make it stop.

'STOP! I know what you're going to do. MONSTER. Guanyin Goddess has eyes and she sees what you do. You will burn in Hell.' A voice, low and hoarse, not mine, hisses loudly through the door and it is directed at the person on the other side.

Speak up. Stand up. Rage against them.

The voice in my head booms loudly.

'MONSTER! MONSTER! MONSTER! STOP this abomination.' The voice has now become mine and I am screaming uncontrollably.

Chapter 34

The door is no longer shaking. I hear a shuffle of feet followed by hurried footsteps backing away. The monster has heard me. Yet the voice in my head continues to speak.

Rage against him. Rage against them.

'Who are you? Show yourself,' I say, turning left and right looking for the owner of the voice. The room pulsates with silence.

I can feel the floor again. I walk to my mattress so I can lie down. I feel dizzy. My temples throb and I massage them to ease the tension. I stroke the Goddess for protection. She starts to sear into my flesh and I try to pull her off. She is stuck but I sense something in me loosening up. A breeze, gentle at first, wafts in through the window. The breeze builds up momentum and I feel a chill in the room. I sit up to pull the cotton bedsheet over me. The breeze is now a strong wind, whipping my hair about. This is when I see her—the Guanyin Goddess. She is a glowing spectre in the distance.

The spectre glides towards me, her face twisted with anger. She rotates around the room like a bottled-up typhoon and I feel the raw wrath that I had felt that night at the outhouse when Ah Poh had her big bleed. A familiar force slides into me through my soles. I start to feel scratches up and down my arms.

A wretched and indescribable kind of wail fills Ah Yoke's room. The spectre starts to speak.

Do not let the outrage continue, Mei. You have the power to stop it. You and Hassan. He tried to help me but I was too proud. Look at me. I am a ghost, hungry to take revenge.

The voice knows me. She looks at me. It is not the Guanyin Goddess. I don't know this face, but it is no longer angry. Tears are streaming down each cheek. Then she screams like a prisoner under torture. I am prickled with anguish and fear. The flesh on my arms feels raw, like someone is scratching me, but when I look at them, there is nothing there.

A vision clear and vivid unfolds before my eyes. Shadows dance on the walls and they take the shape of two humans. I see Eminent Mister Lee. His protruding forehead is unmistakable. A little girl, a mui tsai, is pinned to the corner of her mattress and wedged against the wall. The mui tsai has the same shape as the spectre. The shadow of Lee hovers above her and then the two shadows merge into one.

The howling continues. The room turns slowly like the wheel of a rice mill. The shadows change shapes. This time I see the mui tsai, her tummy round. Number One Madam is striking her with a rattan cane. The mui tsai backs away. She drops on her knees. She curls into a foetal ball, holding her stomach. A baby's cries pierce the humid air.

Don't let them take our babies away. Stop this injustice. Stand up for us.

I feel nauseous. My head is spinning. A pressing ache pulsates where my mole is. I retch and throw up bile. Another shadow appears, this time on the floor, my vomit providing a screen. It's the form of Ah Wan Jie. She is looking back as she cradles a bundle. She starts to run. A baby wails. Squares, triangles and a metal gate. I hear bells pealing softly. Ah Wan Jie's head turns left and right. She places the bundle at the gate and scurries away. The voice in my head is screaming now.

My baby. My baby girl. Give her back to me. You're all murderers. I only wanted to be loved and to be honoured like he had promised me. He promised me that I will not have to worry about being hungry, poor, and destitute anymore.

Chapter 35

I am slicing lemongrass when Ah Chin comes into the kitchen with a message for me. Number One Madam has asked to see me, he says. She's just come home from a round of mahjong with one of her sisters and I am to go up to her bedchamber, Ah Chin relays her message, before I start with dinner. My heart sinks as I know what she will be asking me to do.

'Ah Wan Jie, how is the mui tsai, Ah Poh, doing?' Her words say one thing but her voice is empty of feelings.

'She is weak, Madam, still bleeding.'

Number One Madam is seated at her teak vanity table, a piece of furniture she had brought with her as part of her trousseau. She nods at me as she removes her diamond earrings. I can see her reflection in the vanity mirror. Her face is hard, her lips a tight line. An uncomfortable silence fills the air for a few moments before she continues, her uncaring eyes locked on mine through the mirror. 'Keep giving her the medicine. And when she is better—'

A cockroach takes flight and Number One Madam jumps from her seat, screaming. With quick reflexes that I'd forgotten I possess, I leap to chase the black pest hitting it with a wooden clog until it is pulped into a juicy mess. My right wrist throbs with heat, pulsating with pain. My knees are filled with water again. I would do better seated, but if I were I wouldn't be able to kill the cockroach so easily. I stand there, one foot bare, ignoring the pain in my body and tell the madam that I'll clean up the mess I'd made.

'I'll fetch some newspapers to wrap it up in later, Madam, and get Ah Mei to mop up the mess.'

Number One Madam composes herself, doesn't seem to be bothered by the smashed carcass of the cockroach like I am, and sits back down again. She is wringing her hands like she had done on the night Ah Mei arrived. Her eyes are looking at me through the mirror, but they are seeing something a distance away.

'Ah Mei … you said she was ordinary, didn't you, Ah Wan Jie?'

'Yes, Madam, she is.' I lie again.

I brace myself for a good scolding. The silence is troubling. But when Number One Madam opens her mouth to speak, she changes the subject instead.

'Number Three is pregnant again. Her mui tsai has just informed me.'

I wasn't expecting this. This can only mean one thing: The Eminent Mister Lee will no longer be visiting Number Three Madam. I also know from Ping-chieh that the Eminent Mister Lee no longer visits Number One Madam either, and hasn't for a long time.

'How do you know, Ping-chieh?'

'Aiyo, Ah Wan, it's so obvious. Once a woman has passed a certain age, she is no longer desirable.'

'Number One Madam is hardly an older woman, Ping-chieh. She is younger than me, not yet fifty.' I said in Number One Madam's defence.

Ping-chieh chuckled and said, 'What do you know, Ah Wan! You've never had a man.'

I blushed at her insensitive words. She was right, what man would want to marry me with my stained face?

'Have you seen the way he hungers after the new mui tsai?'

'You mean Ah Mei?'

'Who else, Ah Wan? Who else? She has an arresting face. Nothing escapes this man's eyes, Ah Wan—nothing.'

'I must keep Ah Mei away, then,' I said out loud and Ping-chieh said, 'how can you? His lust trails after him each step of the way.'

'I want you to make some herbal soups for Number Three. She will need some boy-producing herbs. Make sure that the sinseh gets the prescriptions right. I will ask Ping-chieh to write this down for me like she had written out Ah Lian's prescription,' Number One Madam says breaking my memory. Doesn't she mean Ah Poh? I let that slippage rest.

'In any case, we need to make sure that Number Three is healthy enough to produce a boy. A healthy boy, not like the new Number Two's. Ping-chieh will know what to write.'

I know that Number One Madam is embarrassed by her illiteracy. She is not like the late Number Two Madam who was from a prominent Peranakan-Chinese family, the daughter of a rubber tycoon, and schooled. Number One Madam was China-born and from a middle-class merchant family. But she has assimilated well into the Peranakan-Chinese way of life since her marriage to Eminent Mister Lee some twenty years ago.

I sigh inwardly while mentally preparing for the imminent visits to the temple to pray for a boy. Somehow, Number One

Madam has gotten it into her head that it is her responsibility to pray for boys to carry on the Lee name and that I must be the one to accompany her to the temple. I don't know if this is a practice in China because I have not heard first wives doing this for the little wives in the Straits. I wonder why it is so important to Number One Madam if Number Three has a son. Surely, she is not thinking of bringing him up like she did Master Lee?

Perhaps, this pregnancy will be an important one because other than Master Lee and his baby brother, all the Lee offsprings are girls. Another chance to bear a boy to carry on the Lee surname. Another boy is crucial because Number Two's son is sickly. He bleeds easily and has now been prevented from playing outside or with other children. Every knock for him, the sinseh had said, is one knock nearer to nailing down the coffin's lid. It also means that the Lee patriarch will have one less son to venerate him after his demise.

These thoughts churn in my head like a curry gone bad in my stomach. My mind is already on other things when Number One Madam finishes our meeting with harsh and penetrating words.

'When Ah Poh is better, you're to send her to Po Leung Kuk. They will find her a husband who is happy to take soiled goods like her. Master Lee has agreed to this and he will write the matron a letter explaining.'

Soiled goods. Hnh.

'As for Ah Mei, we will need to find her a husband soon. The faster she is out of my hair and away from Eminent Mister Lee, the better.'

Chapter 36

Hassan is already there in the alleyway when I step out from the exit door at the end of the kitchen. It is a balmy night, not unusual for this time of year. We're a few days to April and the night showers have come early this year. It had rained in the afternoon, cooling the temperatures down, making tonight very pleasant. Hassan puts out his candle when I arrive so that it doesn't have to compete with the half-full moon. I take my place beside him on our stone slab in the enveloping duskiness, relieved to be sitting down after hours of standing up doing the ironing.

I am eager to tell Hassan about my vision. As usual he is all ears. My voice is urgent, seeking answers.

'Ah Lian is back, Mei,' he says with a sigh, after I have finished.

I feel his body trembling. Hassan's cries, soft and sad, punctuate the quietness of the night.

'I tried to help her, Mei,' he says in between sobs.

Did Hassan love Ah Lian? Is that why he is crying? Is that why he wouldn't tell me more?

A jealous bile rise from my stomach to the back of my throat. 'You loved her, Hassan. I am not your only moon and star.'

At this, Hassan starts to laugh, his laughter stifled by his sobbing and he starts to hiccup. I feel a strong shame whirling with the intense fury sitting in my chest. *How could Hassan lie to me? How stupid I've been to trust him?*

My slap echoes the outrage I am feeling.

Hassan stops me from hitting him again by holding on to my wrist so tightly that it begins to hurt.

'Mei, stop! Listen to me.' He sounds agitated and desperate. 'Liar!'

'Mei, Ah Lian was my friend.'

'Friend?' I scream at Hassan, not caring if my shouting will wake Ah Wan Jie or someone in the house up.

'A girl and a boy from another race cannot be friends.'

'Wha—? What are you saying, Mei? She was my friend. I tried to help her. Tried to stop her from making a mistake.'

'I don't believe you. Liar!' I shout again, this time slightly louder than before.

'Not so loud, Mei. Listen to me, please.'

I wrestle my left wrist free, rubbing it to ease the ache that Hassan's tight grip had caused. Hassan starts to tell me how he became entangled in Ah Lian's life. They knew each other, used to play together as children, because they had lived in the same kampung in the countryside before Encik Abdullah opened his sundries shop in town and brought Hassan to work for him, moving the family out of the kampung. It was by coincidence that Ah Lian was sold to the Lee household and their paths crossed again when she was sent to Encik Abdullah's to run errands for Ah Wan Jie. He tells me that their kampung was a multi-ethnic one where Malays, Chinese and Indians live together. It is different from mine, which was inhabited by mainly Chinese families, except for a couple of Malay homes. The Malays live in our kampung because both families have members who also work at the gentlemen's club where Aunty Eng cleans the toilets.

'She had delusions that Eminent Mister Lee would marry her.' Hassan finishes the story with this line.

As I piece the jigsaw of information together, I begin to see why Ah Lian's life had turned out the way it did. I see how she became this hungry ghost, floating between Hell and Earth, forever insatiable, always longing, filled with unfulfilled hopes. Suddenly, the shadows make sense.

I don't feel as angry at Hassan now. But I'm still not clear about Ah Lian's mistake.

'Was this her mistake?'

'Yes, Mei, she had let her illusion take her too far. She didn't understand that men like Mister Lee would never take a girl like her seriously.'

'Why? You told me that he promised her marriage. Promised to rescue her. A mui tsai a few doors down just married her master. It's not impossible.'

Hassan sighs and I feel the weight of my question on his shoulder. I don't know why I even asked Hassan why and said what I did, after now knowing what Eminent Mister Lee is capable of.

'A man can promise a girl the world. That's what we do, it's ingrained in us.'

My head spins as I try to make sense of Hassan's words. I don't understand where they had come from. *Why would Hassan say this? He promised to set us free. Did he say this because it is part of his make up as a man? Did he promise to love me because that's what all men do—make empty promises?*

'You have promised me the world, Hassan,' I say, choking on my tears, 'did you mean what you'd said?'

After I say this, I remember Ah Wan Jie's laments about men. Maybe she is right—men are just useless and cannot be trusted. I wish Ma was here to tell me what to do.

Chapter 37

Lee household, April to June 1932

Since Mrs Shirin Fozdar's speech and Mister Pickering's visit to the Lee house, there has been a lot of noise about the need to register mui tsai. This noise has percolated down to the servants at the Lee household through the many activities that have been taking place at the house. They are all centred on Percy Lee since he has established a law firm to advise citizens on their rights as workers. I know this from the shouting matches between Percy Lee and his father, Mister Lee, who is adamant that his son should not be standing up for the rights of coolies, mui tsai and servants.

'Mei, you know, it is hard to be a good human being,' Ah Wan Jie says.

'What do you mean?'

'Well, just look at Master Lee—'

Ah Wan Jie tells me, as we eat our breakfast, that Percy Lee's decision to be a better human being than his father is causing his mother much consternation. Number One Madam is concerned that Mr Tang will call off the marriage because no merchant would want a son-in-law who is more interested in protecting human rights than mercantile interests. But Percy Lee has his ways with Number One Madam, even if he is only an adoptee, not her flesh and blood. I suspect this is why Ah Poh's fate turned out better considering what had happened.

'Ah Poh is no longer going to live with us,' Ah Wan Jie continues.

Ah Wan Jie catches my eye when she tells me that Number One Madam wants to send Ah Poh to the Po Leung Kuk on York Hill to be re-educated. She is no longer to be the responsibility of the Lee household. Another mui tsai will replace Ah Poh, it has been decided. Whether she will be registered or not, I have no idea. Ah Wan Jie has her views about the legal necessity to free mui tsai. Where will they go if not for the benevolence of people like the Lee family, she tells me. I have no answers, only more questions. All I can think about is how Number One Madam has wrenched another little girl from her mother again. The new mui tsai is from Malaysia this time. This means that she is a longer way away from home than I am.

Home.

As I am also responsible for Ah Poh, I am to accompany her to the Po Leung Kuk together with Ah Wan Jie. Before the trip, Ah Wan Jie swore me to silence.

'Ah Poh doesn't know that she will be going there, Mei,' Ah Wan Jie says, her voice sad but urgent, '… make up a story but don't tell her the truth.'

'Why do we need to lie to her, Ah Wan Jie?'

'Not lie, Mei, temper the truth, that's all. What good is it for Ah Poh to know that she's been kicked out of the Lee household.'

'Kicked out?'

'Yes, Mei … what do you think?… you think Madam would continue to keep her here?'

'Yes … I think that Madam should keep her here. She hasn't done anything wrong. It's Number One Madam's responsibility to find Ah Poh a good husband when she is eighteen.'

Ah Wan Jie bites her lower lip and shakes her head. 'What an innocent fool you are, Ah Mei.'

I feel a heat rise up chafing my ears with embarrassment. Maybe I am a fool … especially around men.

'Mei, I know that I am closer to your mother's age than a sister's. So I will tell you one thing that mothers ought to tell all their daughters,' Ah Wan Jie continues, seeing that I haven't said anything.

'Are you willing to listen to a foolish old lady who knows a thing or two about young love.'

I look at Ah Wan Jie. For the first time, I notice that her eyes are light brown and she has a tiny speck of yellow in the white of her right eye. I see strays of grey, poking out from a head of black hair, and a pair of eyebrows peppered with straggly white strands. Today, the stain on her face is flushed a darker shade of pink. Ah Wan Jie's tone is resolute, tinged with sadness. I nod at her to continue.

'A young girl when she starts to become a woman is always naive. Like Ah Lian, like Ah Poh … like … you.'

I see concern in her eyes. They are moist, glistening with pent-up emotion. A tear runs down her left cheek and she sweeps it away hurriedly.

'Let me begin with Ah Poh. She is young, only fourteen in Chinese years. She is not as ambitious as Ah Lian was, she's a simple girl, not very smart in the head.'

I am reeling inside just hearing Ah Wan Jie's impression of Ah Poh. I chew on my lower lip waiting for her to continue.

'She could not stop what was happening to her. Did not have a voice.'

I nod, agreeing with Ah Wan Jie at this point. Ah Poh is a quiet girl, a good girl, does what she is told. Even when she was suffering from pain and blood loss, she never complained.

'She did not make a mistake, as you'd said. But she is now soiled, Ah Mei, do you understand? Number One Madam has nothing to offer the groom's family now—who would marry a girl like Ah Poh?'

'A girl like Ah Poh? Ah Wan Jie—' I say.

'Let me explain. A girl like Ah Poh is only good for one thing now—as a little wife to a man who doesn't care that she is no longer a virgin. There are not many of such men, perhaps only those interested to trade Ah Poh's body for money.'

Ah, the bride price, also her prize. Of course. A boy can sow his wild oats but a girl must remain virginal. A man's body belongs to himself and a woman's to him. Ma had already told me this. I taste the bitter bile that has risen from my stomach to my mouth.

'Now, let's talk about Ah Lian, shall we? You see, all Ah Lian wanted was some security and maybe love, if she's lucky. A fifth wife to a wealthy man is better than being the first wife to a poor man. But, neither guarantees love nor security. A woman with no status must always swallow bitter medicine … must always accept second best …'

Ah Wan Jie nods at me, imploring me to understand. I gulp down the bile. And after a few seconds I nod in return, not in agreement but in an attempt to find out more.

'… you understand? Ah Lian made a mistake and that was to trust an old lizard like Mister Lee and for giving him a prize that he coveted and that she can never claim back. And, you know what's the worst? Both Ah Lian and Ah Poh had no might to stop him.'

I don't understand because I would never want to be the no status wife of a rich man. I want to be a wife to a man who loves me. Yet, I know that I am also a no status girl, with not much might to fight for my freedom. The realization knocks the wind out of me. There are so many things that are not within my control. My heart aches as I think of Hassan. I had left abruptly that night, leaving him sitting there all alone. I want so badly for things to be different.

Do something about it. It's the voice in my head again, interrupting my thoughts. *You have the power.*

My Guanyin pendant feels warm against my skin.

Chapter 38

On the morning of our trip, Ah Poh is brimming with excitement because this is her first time out of the Lee house since she started working there at the age of eight. Her eyes meet mine for a minute seeking assurance, and I sense a small wave of nervousness. I nod slightly at her, nervous too. But I don't let on. Ah Wan Jie flags down a rickshaw, then sends the puller away again on account of his feet, wrapped in cloth.

'Too old, poor man,' she says to me, pointing to the man's feet, 'blistered feet, that's why he wrapped them up.' She flags another down. We climb on to the rickshaw, Ah Poh and I sitting by Ah Wan Jie's feet.

Ah Poh's eyes glow with wonder as the rickshaw passes lalang fields covered by a thick blanket of this tall wheat-like grass. She looks at me and flashes me a big smile as she inhales, taking in the grassy scent. Further along, we pass by all kinds of buildings—temples, churches, mosques, mansions, and she asks what each monument is. Motor cars zoom past emitting gasoline fumes and other rickshaws run past, some slower, others faster. Women in saris, some with their heads wrapped in a flowing scarf, and ladies in cheongsams add a colourful layer to the street scene. Some menfolk are in European suits while some are dressed in singlets and sarongs, some men are wearing turbans and others a songkok—this is a showcase of the multi-ethnic citizens of our nation. Ah Poh's head turns left and right at each passing sight, her questions that are met with no answers turn into a soundscape of amazement.

The Po Leung Kuk sits at the top of York Hill. As we approach the house, Ah Wan Jie explains to Ah Poh the reason for our trip to the house up the hill. For charity, she tells Ah Poh.

'Oh … oh … oh, I know that Ah Ping Yee … used to go there a lot during her days off,' Ah Poh says, '… to help out, she had said. The girls there…they needed a mother figure.' Her voice tingles with delight.

'Yes … yes … Ah Lian … that's what we're going to do there too … help out,' Ah Wan Jie replies in an all too eager voice.

Ah Lian? Surely, Ah Wan Jie must be confused, but I don't say a word. My silence is complicitous, I know, but it is better I keep quiet than speak and give the game away. Ah Poh looks at me and I turn away quickly before she senses my turmoil.

Ah Poh has lost some weight but colour has returned to her oval face. It has been a long road back to health for her. Nobody has broached the subject of Ah Poh's big bleed, save for Percy Lee. Ah Wan Jie and I were having our dinner when Percy Lee brisked into the kitchen two nights ago. He sent Ah Wan Jie away, much to her annoyance and surprise.

'Mother wants to see you, Ah Wan Jie,' he said, 'please can you go to her now.' He sounded different from all the other times that I've heard him speak. His voice had an adult ring to it.

'Yes, Master Lee,' Ah Wan Jie replied, her voice resigned. I watched as she heaved herself up from her stool and ambled away.

As soon as her back was turned to us and she was out of earshot, Percy Lee told me, 'This is for the Po Leung Kuk. Hand it over to the directress in charge, the female Chinese Protectorate. She will know what to do and how to look after Ah Poh so that something like this won't happen again.'

He gave me a large white envelope sealed with wax. The red stamp had three Chinese characters on it. Percy Lee looked at me intently as he handed the packet over. I took it with both hands and he encased them in his. Then, he put his right index finger to his lips. Shh, he said and retrieved another packet from his trouser pocket, pressing it into my hands. This packet was smaller—a brown envelope with no wax seal. It rested on top of the larger envelope.

'This is for you,' he whispered, 'you will need it soon. I will let you know what to do when the time is right. Keep this envelope safely away.'

My eyes burrowed into his. He held my gaze, then nodded his head and turned to leave.

My thoughts of Percy Lee and the brown packet he gave me, which I have hidden under a loose floor board in Ah Yoke's room, occupy me as the rickshaw puller pants up the hill barefoot. The puller's panting made me aware of the bitter work he's doing, and I start to think of Ah Gong who had been a rickshaw puller until he died of an opium overdose. A coolie— someone who exerts bitter effort—that is the lot of a servant's life. I don't know why my thoughts would go to Grandfather. Perhaps I am thinking of men, of all men, of servants, masters, sons, husbands. Is every man selfish and egotistical like Ah Wan Jie had made them out to be? I think of Percy Lee. I remember his words from a while back telling me that *we are all equal.* I think of Hassan. I think of our quarrel and his last words as I stormed away. *You are my Polar Star,* he said, echoing Tagore's poetic words.

* * *

Ah Wan Jie tugs the metal chain attached to an iron bell. Locked behind the corrugated metal gate is a house, an European looking house. Unlike the ornate exteriors of Chinese houses, this building is modern with plain white walls. I hear laughter in the distance but don't know which direction the sounds are coming from. Ah Wan Jie asks the rickshaw puller to wait for us and he parks his vehicle under an *angsana* tree and squats under its umbrella to rest. We stand behind the silver gate for a fair bit of time before a Chinese woman in a black and white samfoo unlocks the chain around the gate, letting us in.

'Welcome to the Po Leung Kuk,' she greets us in a serious but friendly tone, 'step this way and I will take you to the directress.'

We walk along a winding gravel path leading us up towards the building. The sound of pebbles crunching mixes with the echoes of light chatter and laughter coming from a garden in the distance. A line of trees leads us to the front of the house. Beside the building, a group of little girls are playing in a cement courtyard. A woman in a samfoo stands watching them. I see a girl jumping with one leg folded behind her as she hops from one chalk-drawn square to another. She bends to pick up a pebble and throws it on another square and hops again on one foot. I used to play hopscotch in the kampung too, our squares drawn with carbon chips. A group of four girls is seated cross-legged on the grass playing a game of four stones. There is another group skipping with a rope made of rubber bands joined together. Their tinkling laughter makes me feel like a child again.

A little girl is sitting alone on the steps leading up to the front door. She moves to make room for our group, then she looks up and our eyes meet. I see a gentle softness behind a pair of limpid doe-like eyes and I am moved by it.

'Off you go, Po Gek …' the Chinese lady shoos the little girl away, 'don't sit there moping, go and play.'

She is called Precious Jade too. Someone had loved her. The little girl gets up and scampers away, her plaited black hair whipping left and right as she runs off to join her friends. I wonder what life would be like for her when she leaves this half-way home.

Above the front door is a wooden cross. We enter into a large hallway, simply decorated with a round table in the centre. A vase with orchids sits in the middle. A Bible is placed on a stand in front of the vase. Ah Wan Jie is led into another room while Ah Poh and I do as we are told—wait on a bench in the corridor just left of the big hall. Behind us is a cabinet with glass doors. And a quick glance shows me two shelves of books, their spines with a column of Chinese characters. The children's laughter has now turned into chants. I spy a room of girls seated at wooden desks. They are wearing similar clothing—a plain samfoo made of light blue cotton. Their girlish voices are reciting something in English. I have no idea what they're saying. I know it's English because the language I'm hearing is not Malay, Fukien, Mandarin or Cantonese. I listen to their recitations. I wonder what it would be like to speak English properly. Some more minutes pass before I hear a shuffle of footsteps coming towards us. The Chinese lady we met at the gate approaches the bench and holds her hand out to Ah Poh.

'Come with me,' she says, 'follow me and I'll show you around.'

She turns to me and says, 'The directress would like to see you as well.' She gestures towards the door that she had exited from.

I knock lightly and open the door, stepping into someone's office. Ah Wan Jie is standing in front of a wooden desk next to an elderly lady dressed in a cheongsam. From her profile, I see that the elderly lady has black hair, resting on her shoulders. She turns to look at me. Her face is framed by a fringe parted at the centre, showing off a pair of arched eyebrows that have been lightly pencilled in. Her eyes are shaped like a teardrop lying on its side and the corners slope upwards, lifting her features. Her black pupils are windows to a heart of kindness. She has a broad nose—a Southern Chinese nose—and an oval face, a little longer than most. There are no lines on her face like there are on Ah Wan Jie's.

'Ah! Mei Mei,' the lady says, 'Ah Wan Jie has been telling me about you and how you've helped Ah Poh back to health. I hear she is positively glowing. Thank you.'

'Thank you, madam,' I say, unsure how to address her as I make my way to stand next to Ah Wan Jie.

'I'm Mrs Wu,' she says, 'I am in charge of the Po Leung Kuk. Master Percy Lee has been very kind with his support of our work here, and that is why Ah Poh has been sent to us. Ah Wan Jie is not unfamiliar with our work either, I'm sure you already know. Her time and generous monthly donations have benefited many of our girls.'

Is that why Ah Wan Jie disappears for hours on end every Saturday afternoon? I glanced quickly to my side, but Ah Wan Jie's eyes stare straight ahead. Mrs Wu continues for a bit more about the importance of volunteers and donations before

I am reminded of Percy Lee's wax-sealed envelope. I unbutton my collar and reach under my samfoo top, where I had stuffed the padded envelope into my bra strap under my left armpit. The envelope is slightly damp and I feel self-conscious handing it over to Mrs Wu.

'Sorry … from … from Master Lee,' I say awkwardly, extending the envelope to Mrs Wu, aware that Ah Wan Jie's eyes are on me.

'Thank you, Mei. Please convey my thanks to Master Lee and to the family,' Mrs Wu says taking the envelope from me gently. She places it on a pile of papers sitting on top of her desk.

Ah Wan Jie gives a little cough and mentions Ah Poh.

'Ah yes, let's talk about Ah Poh. As requested in Nyonya Lee's letter, I will see to it that Ah Poh is well looked after. We will teach her some life skills that she will need for employment, for marriage and motherhood. She will learn to read in both Chinese and English. She is still young enough to get some schooling in her—'

'About the scratches, Mrs Wu,' Ah Wan Jie interrupts. 'Ah Poh scratches herself.'

'Ah-yes. The letter did mention this too,' Mrs Wu continues without any irritation. Ah Wan Jie has just interrupted a woman of high status and I am expecting a harsh word from Mrs Wu. Instead, she gestures to two chairs in front of her desk, asking Ah Wan Jie and me to take a seat.

'Why don't you sit down and I will explain some things to you both. It's better that you understand.' She walks around to take her seat opposite us.

I am looking at Mrs Wu when I see the window behind her, its shutters opening out to the garden. Beyond the window is a weeping willow with branches cascading over a well, boarded up. Something stirs inside of me—an oppressive sensation of sadness. I feel the prickling of goosebumps on my arms.

Mrs Wu thanks Ah Wan Jie kindly for bringing up Ah Poh's injuries. I am brought back to the room on hearing this. Mrs Wu's voice is even, matter of fact, as she explains that self-harming is a sign of trauma and distress. There are many girls who have come to the Po Leung Kuk with similar injuries to Ah Poh. Many also enter the half-way home with injuries inflicted on them by their owners, she continues.

'Ah Poh has suffered much and it is right that she is now under the care of the Po Leung Kuk,' Mrs Wu says.

I expect her to continue by mentioning what Mister Lee has done. But instead, she says something else, 'this is the work we do at the Po Leung Kuk, after all …'

Mrs Wu is beaming from ear to ear as she carries on with conviction in her voice, '… and Ah Poh will be mended, be of marriageable quality again. We will make sure that she forgets her past when she is ready to be married to a suitable family. They will marvel at the things she can do beyond cleaning. She will be able to cook, sew, look after babies …'

Clean. Cook. Look after babies. Is this what all girls are destined to do? I know that Mrs Wu means well; her voice is soft, gentle, not judgemental. But, what I am most unnerved by was the way she had talked about Ah Poh. *Mended?* What an absurd way of referring to poor Ah Poh. It is as if she is not a person, a girl, but a piece of furniture or a broken bowl, something that can be fixed when broken.

Chapter 39

On our ride home, I ask Ah Mei to tell me why Master Lee had given her the sealed envelope instead of me. I can only guess that it was filled with a wad of money, looking at its shape—thick and rectangular like a book.

'Was it money, Mei?'

Ah Mei is reticent, shrugging her shoulders as she sits by my feet. I see from her profile that she is resolute. But I am determined too.

'Mei, why you, not me?'

She turns her back to me, deflecting my question, looking towards the rickshaw puller instead. I am immensely annoyed. Ah Mei is with me but her mind is somewhere else.

Well, at least, I was made in charge of the letter. I am still the highest-ranking servant in the Lee household, if not Number One Madam would not have entrusted me with such an important letter.

'Take this letter with you to the Po Leung Kuk,' Number One Madam said, flinging the letter at me. Her temper is uncontrollable these days. Her hands were balled into fists and she was seething, glaring at me.

'Master Lee has written something for the directress and he wants you to be in charge of it.'

She spat the words out. Then paused before she started to talk about the new mui tsai and reminding me about my duties again.

The new mui tsai was waiting for me in the kitchen. Ah Chin had just deposited her there as Ah Mei and I had just started our dinner. Ah Mei was in the middle of asking her to join us for dinner when Master Lee walked in unexpectedly. Master Lee glanced quickly at the girl but didn't say anything. Then, he told me to go and see his mother and started to speak to Mei. His voice was too soft for me to hear what he's telling Ah Mei.

My life as a Lee servant continues as usual even though Ah Poh has been swapped with a new mui tsai. Since that day, I have been instructing the new girl as is my duty. I am not as dedicated with this one, I'll say, because I have other things on my mind. I am bothered that Ah Mei has been avoiding me since our visit to the Po Leung Kuk a month ago. When I enter the kitchen, she leaves, mumbling excuses. She hardly speaks to the new mui tsai but would pick out an extra piece of chicken for her at meal times. She tells the mui tsai to eat and be strong. I hear concern as well as confidence in Ah Mei's voice.

The new girl has a mousy face with a sharp chin, all gaunt, and her skin is sallow. She is a scrawny thing and has small fearful eyes. I am guessing she's about seven or eight years old, which is the typical age when they're sold. I know she's come from a kampung in Malaysia and speaks Fukien. Ah Chin had told me this. The way he looked at me after depositing the mui tsai told me that he didn't think she would last long. Ah Chin is a kind man. Our paths would be so different if we were both born in a different family and in a different time. I dismiss whatever tender thoughts I have for him; what's the point of holding on to them?

The mui tsai, Ah Choo, is streaked with rattan marks; the long finger-like strokes on her arms are blue-black, so the beating must have taken place some time ago. I wonder what she had done to deserve such a pelting. But, I haven't the energy to pursue the matter.

The sleeping arrangement remains the same. Ah Mei sleeps in Ah Yoke's room and the mui tsai with me. Since our trip to the Po Leung Kuk, Ping-chieh decided to retire and has left the Lee household for good. Number One Madam had no choice but to let Ping-chieh leave since as a paid servant, she has rights. It was a sad day for me because I know I will miss her wisdom. The new mui tsai is my only companion and she's not much of one, crying every night to go home. What can I do?

I am now a bona fide majie, a celibate female servant, like Ping-chieh. I can't officially join the sisterhood because I am not from the same village in China. I was born here in the Straits. Yet, Ping-chieh had taken me through the hair-combing ritual, making me swear before the Goddess Guanyin that I will remain unmarried. As a celibate woman, I can adopt a daughter one day. A daughter to look after me when I'm old, Ping-chieh said. Ping-chieh has adopted one from the Po Leung Kuk.

The house is throbbing to a different energy now that Ah Poh has left. It is as if a heavy fog has lifted and we are not shrouded by darkness anymore. Ah Mei's energy has also changed and I don't feel that I can rein her in now: I don't need to ask her to run errands for me as she takes the initiative herself.

'I'm off to the shops, Ah Wan Jie, we need some dried goods and rice.' Her voice sounds like she is in charge. I know why she is eager to be busy this way. I am too tired to stop her.

Chapter 40

'I saw it, saw the well,' I tell Hassan a month after our trip to the Po Leung Kuk. This is the first time we've had any time to be together.

'The well? What well, Mei? ... you're not making sense.'

It's true, I haven't been making much sense lately, even to myself. The trip to the Po Leung Kuk has stirred something in me. The girls living there, what would really happen to them? Who would want them? I didn't get to say goodbye to Ah Poh and I know I would never see her again. Would she be married off to a good family? Would she be able to forget her past? Ah Wan Jie's work at Po Leung Kuk, that Mrs Wu had mentioned, made me wonder about Ah Wan Jie's intention regarding mui tsai. I wonder too how involved she was in Ah Lian's fate. I know that she saw the well too. I felt her energy change when she sat down beside me.

For nearly a month now, my sleep is light and my dreams are lucid, vivid. In my dreams, I see the shape of a mui tsai falling into the well at the Po Leung Kuk. Black water spills out of this well and the smell of stagnant water is strong. This stench assaults me and I wake abruptly to scratch marks on my arms. I have not been able to make any sense of these dreams nor understand why I am viciously scratching myself. I try to read for signs in my tea leaves, but one can't read one's own fate. Even though I know this, I try nonetheless.

I am also wondering what to do with the packet that Percy Lee had given me. He said to wait for him to tell me what to do. Out of curiosity, I opened it on the night after our visit to the Po Leung Kuk. There was enough money in there to last me a lifetime. I was so shocked that I stuffed the wad of notes back in its case and placed the envelope under the floor boards again. I pinched myself in case this was all part of my lucid dreams.

'Nothing, Hassan, just a well at the Po Leung Kuk, that's all.' I let my words hang in the air and change the subject. 'Just wondering about Ah Poh.'

Hassan holds me to him and whispers, 'It's ok, Mei. It's ok, you'd done your best for Ah Poh. She will be fine, I feel it in my bones.'

Hassan and I are speaking like old times again. On the way down York Hill, I told myself that I must not judge all men using the same yardstick. Everyone is capable to act differently and to tar every person with the same brush is just not right. I am Hassan's Polar Star. He is my world. I need to hold on to that truth. I must find a way to break free so that we can be together.

So, I start to tell Hassan about Mrs Fozdar's visit to the Lee house.

'You saw her? Really?'

'Yes, Hassan, really.' Annoyance creeps up my neck and I am surprised by this emotion. I shake it off, focusing on what I want to tell Hassan.

'Ah Yoke and I saw her from behind the latticed shutter. Then I went in to the Guest Hall to serve the tea and cakes.'

'What do you think she's doing there, Mei?'

I tell Hassan what I heard and what I understood. The conversation was all in English, so not everything was clear to me. But it was cordial as there was no shouting. Both Mrs Fozdar and Percy Lee seem to agree with each other as there was a lot of head nodding. I mention that I heard the words mui tsai, ordinance and rights again. Hassan nods. He grins. And he holds me tight.

'So, I guess she must be there to talk about freeing mui tsai, Hassan.'

'Wah seh!' Hassan cheers in Fukien and gives a victory pump. Then, he lifts me off my feet. He twirls around. I feel like I am flying.

'I have a good feeling, Hassan.'

After I said this, I had a brain wave, an idea: I know what I can do with the money Percy Lee has given me. I don't need to wait for him to tell me what to do.

Chapter 41

I am baking the final layer of the cake lapis and preparing a chiffon mixture for another cake. My crooked fingers ache from holding the cake tin. My knuckles and joints are still swollen even with all the remedies I've been taking and today my whole body is aching as well.

There seems to be plenty of guests these days. Master Lee has been busy entertaining men and women, talking and discussing. And guests must be fed which means more work than usual. There has also been a lot of shouting between Master Lee and his father. The shouts reverberate through the house and everyone is uneasy. It is never any good when a son starts to talk back to his father.

Eminent Mister Lee has been unwell on top of it. The sinseh has been to see him a few times now. Today's visit is his fifth in two weeks. Eminent Mister Lee is complaining that his chest pains are getting worse and of headaches that he says started in the morning. The headaches are a new addition to the sickness that is ailing Eminent Mister Lee.

As soon as I'm done with the cake mixture, I start on preparing the medicinal broth for the old master. After opening the packet, I take a sniff of this batch and detect something slightly different about the remedy, though the herbs look the same. To be sure, I sniff again, putting my nose closer this time. There it is, a more potent scent—bitter with a whiff of *buah keluak*. I am somewhat suspicious, because the keluak nut is poisonous, but the sinseh is an honest man. Perhaps he made this batch stronger for a good reason and I'm sure that if it's the keluak he's added, it must be fit for ingestion. But something still doesn't sit quite right as I sprinkle the herbs into the claypot. Have I missed something here—when did the remedy change? Did it change? Is *buah keluak even* medicinal? Oh well, never mind, because what can I do? I have just done filling the claypot with eight bowls of water with the herbs submerged in it when I hear Number One Madam calling for me. Since Ah Poh's big bleed, Number One Madam has taken to ringing a bell to summon me, like how she used to call for Ah Poh. It takes me a while to get to Mr Lee's chambers. The wind trapped in my knees makes it hard to climb those steep stairs quickly. When I get there, I see the sinseh writing out another prescription for which Ah Mei will have to collect. Number One Madam seems agitated. Her voice is strained as she tells me what the sinseh has said and what I need to do. Eminent Mister Lee's symptoms have changed and I must boil the herbs for longer this time. I fear that nothing good will come out of this no matter what new medicines the sinseh is prescribing. But it is not my place to say anything. I take the prescription from the sinseh and amble away in pain.

'Ah Mei, go and fetch the herbs for Eminent Mister Lee.' I say, giving Mei the prescription as soon as I am back in the kitchen. I am perspiring. My head is all wet like I've just had a bath. The weather is turning once more as the monsoon winds change course again. The air is hot and muggy.

'Of course,' Ah Mei replies, 'but nothing seems to be working, Ah Wan Jie. I mean the sinseh has come a few times now and you've made Mister Lee herbal potions many times now too.'

'I know, Mei, it is strange that the remedies have not been working. The sinseh is good at his job. He's been with the family a long time … Old Mister Lee used to see him as well. He lived to a good old age … ah … he's a good man, the senior Lee, and—'

I am about to say how good the sinseh has been with Ah Lian then Ah Poh too, prescribing the right medicines for both girls, but decide against mentioning both their names. I wonder if I should mention my doubts and suspicions about Eminent Mister Lee's last packet of herbs, but thought against it too. Instead, I share with Mei my doubts about the sinseh's prescription for me. 'Well, the pangolin scales he prescribed for me hasn't done anything for my arthritis … there's still wind trapped in my bones making my fingers swell and ache, and now my knees.'

Then I remember that the sinseh's prescription for the late Mister Lee's eye trouble didn't do anything either. Old Mister Lee's eyes grew whiter and whiter and his vision cloudier and cloudier even with all the herbal potions I'd made for him.

'… perhaps, the sinseh doesn't know everything, after all.'

Mei doesn't reply. She takes a parasol and leaves for the medical hall with the new prescription.

I throw out the suspicious batch and wash the clay pot out ready for the new prescription. Then I put the tin of chiffon mixture in the oven. I don't have to watch the oven with this cake as I have to with the layered lapis. A sudden rush of heat wells up inside me. I sit and fan myself, relieved to have some minutes of rest. Ah Mei is not gone long before Ah Choo comes running frantically into my kitchen. Her face is white as a sheet, like she has seen a ghost.

'Number One Madam ... she wants you, Ah Wan Jie ... something ... something has happened upstairs.'

I heave myself up with a sigh and rush up the stairs with Ah Choo as fast as my arthritic knees can take me. Ah Choo takes me to Eminent Mister Lee's chamber. Number One Madam is slapping her husband's face, trying to wake him up. She is crying in panic and begging the old man not to leave her. She calls out to the sinseh, who unfortunately has already left.

'Go, Ah Choo, go ask Ah Chin to get the sinseh right away ... go ... go now,' I whisper hard and urgently. The poor girl scurries away in fright.

Eminent Mister Lee is frothing at the mouth and he is shaking and twitching like a man possessed. I have only seen this once when Chandra the gardener went into a trance, thinking that he was Shiva, the Hindu God of Destruction. I glance at the wall clock across from Mister Lee's bed. It's twenty to four in the afternoon. Seeing that Number One Madam's effort isn't doing much, I accompany her in patting Eminent Mister Lee's cheeks, trying to wake him up, coaxing him back to our world.

The clock strikes four, the hour of death, and Ah Mei arrives with the Eminent Mister Lee's new prescriptions. She walks boldly into Eminent Mister Lee's room and stands next to me, the herbal packet in her hand. What possessed her to bring the packet of herbs up to Eminent Mister Lee's room, I will never know. I turn to give her a warning look, conscious of Number One Madam's instructions to keep Ah Mei away from her. She is staring at Eminent Mister Lee, her face straight and hardened, her eyes uncaring. She gasps softly and then lets out a long sigh, mumbling something under her breath.

'Leave,' I whisper, 'Madam, doesn't want you here.'

By the time the sinseh arrives again, Eminent Mister Lee has stopped twitching but saliva is dripping from his drooping mouth. His eyes stare vacantly ahead. The sinseh feels for Eminent Mister Lee's pulse, lifts his eyelids to take a look at his *hun*, his spirit. He turns to look at Number One Madam, shakes his head, saying, 'Eminent Mister Lee has had a stroke. There is nothing more I can do here. I am sorry. I don't know how long he will be in this state, his essence half gone.' At that point, Number One Madam starts to cry again, saying, 'Ah Pek, Ah Pek, you cannot leave me now.'

She collapses into a chair by Mister Lee's bed, hiding her face in her hands. It is as if the Eminent Mister Lee has died.

Chapter 42

When I arrive back at the kitchen, Ah Wan Jie was nowhere to be found. I take the packet up to the sleeping quarters. I could've left it on the work table for Ah Wan Jie, but I felt a strong urge to go upstairs. As soon as I am at the top of the stairs, I hear Number One Madam wailing. A desperate cry. It is bone chilling. Mister Lee lies catatonic in his bed. I stand at the entrance to his chambers and stare at him. His lips are drooping, his face contorted. He stares straight ahead, not really moving except for a couple of times when he jerks and twitches. A frothy trail of saliva drips down his stubbled chin.

Still trying to catch my breath, I step into Mister Lee's bedchamber and find a spot next to Ah Wan Jie. She is standing by Mister Lee's bed, facing Number One Madam. The madam doesn't see me. She is grief-stricken, begging Mister Lee not to leave her. The sinseh arrives shortly after me. He comes in and stands next to Number One Madam. She moves aside to give him room. The sinseh opens his medical bag and takes out some acupuncture needles and some glass cups. He looks flustered and harried as he moves closer to Mister Lee. I don't blame him; he had just left the Lee house and is now back again. The sinseh holds Mister Lee's wrist and then puts one ear to his mouth as if listening for Eminent Mister Lee to say something. The sinseh stays in this bent position a few seconds more before straightening himself. Then, he turns to Number One Madam, who is still crying into her hands, and addresses her.

'The Eminent Mister Lee is seventy in Chinese years,' the sinseh says, 'every decade after one's sixtieth year is considered fortuitous. The Emiment Mister Lee is lucky to have this long a life. In my experience, when a man's hun is between Earth and Heaven, his essence is half gone. There is nothing more I can do here. Let's see if he has some spirit left in him to come back to this world.' These words don't comfort Number One Madam whose sobs, now louder, continue to permeate the quiet of the bedchamber.

At this point, Ah Wan Jie hisses at me to leave the bed chamber. I want to go but my legs feel heavy as if they're nailed to the floor boards. The packet of herbs in my right hand feels like a stone. I watch the sinseh pack his bag, putting away his set of acupuncture needles and the glass cups. *There is nothing more I can do here.* I glance at the sinseh as he makes his way out of Mister Lee's bedroom. Our eyes meet as he passes me and for a couple of seconds, I see the man with the cloudy eye in the sinseh's face, the same one that has been following me around for almost a year. The sinseh smiles at me. Goosebumps mushroom up my arms.

I turn around to look at the entrance, my gaze following the sinseh's back as he walks out of the room and towards the stairs. I wait for him to turn and look at me, so that I can see if he is really the man with the glass eye. The sinseh continues down the stairs and disappears around the corner where the stairway turns, and a new emotion I've not felt before fills my every pore. It is a sensation of release like when I've managed to prise open the lid sealed tightly around a clay jar. This sensation gives way to a sense of euphoria. For the first time I don't feel scared on seeing the man with the glass eye. Instead, I feel free. I know that Mister Lee will have no hold over me anymore. *Gone at last.*

'Come let's go downstairs ... there's not much we can do here now,' Ah Wan Jie says, breaking the spell.

Chapter 43

Singapore town, 1932 to 1933

'Here's your pay, Mei,' Percy Lee says, handing me a wax-sealed package.

'Thank you, Master Lee.' I take the packet and write my name on a piece of paper he gives me.

As the eldest son, Percy Lee is now fully in charge of the Lee household and business. Mister Lee lies in bed, staring straight ahead, his eyes vacant, a living corpse. Number One Madam has left the day-to-day running of the house to her step-son, even the care of the mui tsai. She is distraught. Ah Wan Jie says that Number One Madam goes from muttering softly to herself and shouting out at shadows on the wall. Ah Wan Jie has been busy taking care of her needs, so I am doing most of the cooking now. It's simple food as Number One Madam hasn't much of an appetite, Mister Lee only eats a bowl of rice gruel twice a day, and Percy Lee doesn't fuss about what he eats. As for Ah Yoke, she eats what she is given.

'Thank you, Mei, for the work you do around the house. Because you're cooking too, I've made sure to pay you a little more.'

As Percy Lee is now responsible for the mui tsai, he has made sure that we are all registered, following the law, something he calls the Mui Tsai Ordinance of 1932. Percy Lee says I now have rights like Ah Wan Jie and Ah Ping Yee. I am now paid a monthly wage like Ah Wan Jie, and I am free to leave the Lee house to find another job if I wanted to, like Ah Ping Yee could. Though this is good news, I am still a lowly servant. Number One Madam can dismiss me at her whim, even if Percy Lee follows the rules.

As for Ah Ping Yee, Percy Lee takes care of her by giving her some money every month so she can continue to live with her adopted daughter in a rental in Chinatown. She now has nothing to worry about. Percy Lee told me that Ah Ping Yee is more than just a nanny to him. She has been like a mother he never had, comforting him in the early days after his own mother's death and passing on sagely advice and wisdom whenever he needed it.

'She even cried when I left for England,' he said, 'this is the least I can do. I will look after her until she departs this world.'

When I think of what Percy Lee is doing for mui tsai and for Ah Ping Yee, I am comforted to know that not all men are bad men. Yet, I don't want to have to depend on Percy Lee, like Ah Ping Yee, for the rest of my life. I make a mental note to let Percy Lee know how his good deeds have changed me. But, Percy Lee is so busy running the household, advocating for workers' rights and taking care of the family's business that I hardly see him. His wedding has also been put on hold due to his father's health. Like me, he's having to cope with a lot of changes.

Change has been the biggest uncertainty in my life since I came to live with the Lees. Meeting Hassan was the biggest change, I would say. Another transformation is being paid for my services. Even Ah Wan Jie has sensed this.

'Now that you're earning a wage, your life will change, Mei. I wish you all the best.'

'Thank you, Ah Wan Jie.'

But I know that there are more changes yet to come. The phoenixes I embroider on new bibs show me this. Each stitch making up the feathers of this magical bird is a stich bringing me closer to a new chapter.

Each month when Percy Lee hands me an envelope with my wages in it, I feel happy and relieved, but the niggling feeling of not wanting to depend on him lingers. Percy Lee has taught me how to write my name in Chinese so that I can write it on a piece of paper he gives me when he hands me my pay. Being able to put strokes to my name fills me with a sense of power, something I've never felt before.

'This is your signature, Mei,' Percy Lee told me, 'it makes it official that you're receiving a wage. It's in the records.'

I showed Hassan how I can print my Chinese name last night and he wrote my name in English next to it. *Lim Mei Mei.* And then next to this, he wrote *Hassan Mohamed.* We giggle like silly children while saying our names together. Lim Mei Mei and Hassan Mohamed. Hassan Mohamed and Lim Mei Mei.

I know that Hassan and I will have to face many challenges ahead as well. Our union breaks every clause in the rule book. But I believe that our love for each other crosses the different oceans in this world, and is the bridge that will bring our two cultures together. I know Hassan sees this too. I trust him implicitly. I let Hassan kiss me without pushing him away.

I trust Percy Lee too, but I don't want to have to depend on goodwill because goodwill doesn't come all the time, and is dependent on so many things I can't know. What I do know is that there must be something else I can do, must do, to secure my own future, to secure my future with Hassan. I am determined to do this on my own, to build that magpie bridge that would take me and Hassan to freedom.

I need a plan.

Chapter 44

How time has flown by. Ping-chieh's little adopted daughter is now almost twelve. Ping-chieh looks well. Retirement has done her a world of good. I'm sure that the happiness in her face is caused by more than just what a good girl her daughter is. The little girl is good, truth be said, and cute too, with chubby cheeks and a healthy glow. Ah Ping-chieh said that her daughter had come from Malaysia, from a tin-mining town. She was sold for two pieces of silver to a Straits Chinese family in Penang, before making her way to Singapore in a fishing boat, after the Penangnite family became tired of her. Ping-chieh had found her at the Po Leung Kuk, left there by some kind soul who had rescued the girl from a market, where fish, vegetables and little girls were traded. This mui tsai had quite a journey, passed from one set of hands into another, with nobody really caring what would happen to her.

But looking at her now, you couldn't tell. I'm so happy that both mother and daughter are doing so well. Ah Ping-chieh has always rented a small room in a shophouse down in Chinatown, which she continues to share with another majie like her. The room is a box but between her, her daughter and the majie, they manage to live together harmoniously, sharing a double-decker bed. Ping-chieh and her daughter, whom she has named Ah Mooi, sleep on the bunk below, while their roommate takes the top bunk. The room-mate works for a family living a distance away, so is rarely around.

'So, we practically have the place to ourselves when Ah Lan is at work. She works for a family in the East, and it's a long journey back to Big Town. Coming back once a month is all she can afford.' Ping-chieh explained as she poured me a cup of lukewarm tea.

'Well, thanks for visiting again, Ah Wan. You're a good friend.' Ping-chieh said to me when I visited her before the start of Ghost Month.

The room was dimmer than usual. It's late in the afternoon and the sun was hiding behind a cloud. The thin muslin curtains had been pulled together and peeping from behind them were vertical metal bars securing the window. It was the first time I noticed them. The few times I'd visited in the past, Ping-chieh had me sitting on their bed with my back to the window. The bed is next to the window with the top bunk close to the ceiling. Ah Lan must feel like she is in a coffin sleeping up there. These morose thoughts broke away at the sound of Ping-chieh's voice.

'My Ah Mooi will start school soon.'

I sipped my cup of weak tea, sitting on a low stool facing her and Ah Mooi, in pain but also brimming over with happiness. Low stools are not good for my knees, I know, but Ping-chieh has bad knees too. Both Ah Mooi and her are seated on the lower bunk of their double-decker bed. Ah Mooi is holding her mother's hand which is resting on her right lap. I can see them like this twenty, thirty years from now.

In the middle of our conversation, Ah Ping-chieh reached over to the window behind her and pulled the shutters together, leaving just a gap for air. The stench from the squatting toilet below was so strong that she had to light an incense coil placing it under the bed to ward off the nasty sulphuric smell. With the window ajar, it was beginning to feel stuffy. So I fanned myself.

'Hah—it does get better later on in the day when the cooking starts. Better fumes of garlic and ginger, I know. The incense should take away the stink,' Ping-chieh said, after blowing out the match.

'No, no, it's fine, Ping-chieh. Where would you send Ah Mooi to study?'

'Well, there aren't many schools that would take girls, as you know. But I found one run by some women from a Christian mission. It's near the Small Town, up on Mount Sophia. Ah Mooi will have to walk some, but she can start early each day.'

'That's wonderful news, Ping-chieh. I wish I knew how to read and write.'

'I know, Ah Wan, I know. But we mustn't look back, always forward.' Ping-chieh said with conviction.

'Yes, yes, Ah Mooi and her generation are the future.'

'I think so too. It's a small school and they have respect for girls. The school teaches their girls the values of charity, devotion and patience.' Ping-chieh hugged Ah Mooi as she said this. I watched her pinching Ah Mooi's nose and my heart melted from the love that passed between them.

'I can't wait to study, Ah Wan Yee,' Ah Mooi said, her face glowing with hope. I noticed that her thick black hair had been combed thoroughly and braided into two plaits, and I couldn't help but sigh aloud. Smiling at Ah Mooi, I pinched her right cheek gently in encouragement.

'Patience is what we need a lot of, Ah Wan, for change to happen ... for good change to happen,' Ping-chieh continued. Another deep sigh escaped from me because this is so true.

'By the way, how is Ah Mei?'

'Ah Mei is doing well. She sews in the kitchen now. I don't mind since she spends so much time there anyway ... you know, with Number One Madam needing my attention and all. I don't mind mostly because it's better for a girl to have a skill.'

'Yes, you're right about girls having skills. Ah Mei will go far, I see the talent she has with the needle.'

'Yes, she has talent there.'

Perhaps that was why I felt I had to rein Ah Mei in. I was jealous of her talent. But I don't speak this out loud because I know that I can't and mustn't.

'Number One Madam must be so scared. The old man is all she has, she depends on him for everything. It can't be a good thing for her to watch Mister Lee's life ebbing away, with no security for her future.'

'Yes, she's having a hard time, Ping-chieh. But she is lucky to have a son like Master Lee. He's not her flesh and blood, but he's a good son. He will take care of her, I'm sure. Not every step-son is like him.'

'Yes, he is a good man.'

'By the way, Master Lee is now paying Ah Mei a wage. It's the law, he told us.'

Ping-chieh nodded and took a sip of her tea. Then, she gave Ah Mooi twenty cents and told her to go and buy some mung bean cakes.

'We must celebrate because this is a step towards progression. Mui tsai working for a wage and no longer enslaved is a mark of modernity and a sign of a healthy society.'

'Yes, you're right, Ping-chieh, as always. Soon all mui tsai will rise from the fire a powerful and liberated phoenix.'

Ping-chieh looked at me and smiled. Her eyes are wet with tears.

Chapter 45

It's the Hungry Ghost Month once more. Yesterday marked the day I came to live in this house two years ago. The kitchen table is full of ghost food and Ah Wan Jie has started to take the Hell notes and ingots to the back garden. I tuck a packet of joss sticks under my left armpit and pick up the platter of bananas for the hungry ghosts. The bananas will be placed under the frangipani tree by the outhouse. The incense smoke will guide the spirits home. Walking towards the back garden, I squint to remember Ah Mah's face, Ma's caresses, and Huat's boyish grin, recalling the visions and heeding Ah Lian's voice urging me not to forget. I see Ah Mah preparing the food for the spirits and burning paper money for Ah Gong and Tua Ko right now. Ma is stoking the fire and Huat is playing nearby. Red candles mark the temporary altars on the ground and plates of food and cakes by these altars invite the spirits to a feast. I lick my lips and swallow the memories and savour the tastes of my old home— ginger, garlic, fermented soy beans, salted duck eggs and pickled mustard greens.

Ah Wan Jie is already at the back of the Lee garden, near the outhouse, getting ready for the rituals for the Ghost Month.

'Ah Mei, help me with the food, will you?' Ah Wan Jie says, 'just make sure we have everything. There are a few new ghosts to feed this year.'

A whole chicken for the ancestors and a platter of mantou buns for the children are ready for them to feast on when the gates of Hell open. I add the bunch of bananas to the feast. I arrive just before Ah Choo joins us.

'Number One Madam wants me to take part in the rituals this year,' Ah Choo says. She looks from Ah Wan Jie to me as if asking our permission.

Number One Madam wants her to burn paper ingots for the departed souls of new Number Two Madam and her son, the stillborn son of Number Three, and Ah Lian. Ah Wan Jie raises her eyebrows at the mention of Ah Lian's name. She locks eyes with me. I shrug.

'This is what we do, Ah Choo. Watch and follow,' Ah Wan Jie says, feeding the fire with some Hell notes.

As Ah Choo follows by throwing some paper ingots into the fire, I say a prayer for the souls of all abandoned mui tsai. Ah Wan Jie also throws a pile of paper ingots into the spitting flames chanting a prayer at the same time. Then she starts to address her mother, father and ancestors, asking for their protection. I fan out some paper dollars and throw the spirit money into the pyre as well. I ask Ah Gong to look after the family and pray for Tua Ko to rest in peace. Then, for the first time, I put some money in the smokestack for Ah Lian. I whisper her name. I say thank you for showing me the truth, for showing me the injustice that all mui tsai have to endure. I promise her that I will find a way to break these bonds of oppression. I reassure her spirit that peace has finally come—she can rest in peace because I have a plan. I also have a dream, I whisper to her and the universe.

Since Mister Lee's illness, my supernatural visions have lessened. But I still have moments when I am so angry that I start to see black shadows dancing and darting out at me until a pressing ache starts at the nape of my neck. When these moments descend, the only way I can get out of this fugue is to focus on my dream. On good days, waves of relief flow through me because I know that Mister Lee is no longer a threat, helpless as he is prostrated in his bed. I have been sleeping peacefully and deeply since. As for the man with the cloudy eye, he has disappeared completely. The more I focus on my dream, the clearer my personal vision is for my future and the future of mui tsai and girls like me.

The year of Mister Lee's stroke, I started doing some business on the side. I took some of the money that Percy Lee had given me and bought some good-quality cotton, which I cut into squares for hankies and ovals for bibs. Along with the bales of cotton, I also invested in a pair of tailor's scissors, which are sharp and precise, sliding through the cloth neatly. From the colourful spools of thread, which I had invested well in, I would choose the right colours to embroider peonies and goldfish on the square pieces of cotton for handkerchiefs. On the oval pieces, I would embroider phoenixes, using gold and red yarns, and turn these pieces into bibs. Then, I'd take the hankies and bibs to Hassan who has persuaded Encik Abdullah to put them up for sale in his sundries shop. For this, I would give Encik Abdullah a little commission.

Two days before the rituals, before my eighteenth birthday, I took my bundle of needlework to Encik Abdullah myself.

'Ah Mei, you are quite a business woman, I see,' Encik Abdullah said, his eyes twinkling.

I noticed how Encik Abdullah sees me for the first time since I met him. A business woman, he said. I smiled and gave him his commission.

'You will make Hassan a good wife, I can see that,' he added, echoing my plans to leave the Lee household to marry his nephew. This won't be long.

'I will be doing more than this, Pak Abdullah,' I said, 'I plan to open up a shop where I will make clothes for ladies, embroidering motifs and patterns on their dresses.'

'Hah ... ah ... good, good, a business woman, like I said ... Hassan, Hassan, did you hear, boy?' Hassan grinned and winked at me. And in front of his uncle, he hugged me and lifted me off my feet.

Freedom.

I don't tell Pak Abdullah or Hassan of my dream.

I want to set up a sewing school so that I can teach other girls to make beautiful clothes. So that they will know their worth through what they can do. I hold on to that dream because I want to keep it a surprise. I have the money that Percy Lee has given me to do this and I have saved some more from the earnings I am getting from the hankies and bibs. And then when I've made and saved enough money, I will find a way to return Percy Lee the cash he has given me. A loan must be repaid.

I sew only at night when all my chores are done. I pull the needle in and out and see the shapes forming, shapes of good luck, good health and abundant wealth, as Ah Yoke's light snores fill the room. I no longer have to worry about using a raffia string to lock us both in, lock me in. On breezy nights, I stitch by natural light, sitting on the spot of moonlight by the window. This helps me save on candles as well.

'I am so proud of you, my moon and star,' Hassan said when he saw the new batch of hankies and bibs. They're selling well.

A Chinese woman bought up the last batch the other day, all of them at once, Hassan said. There are not many in a batch, only eighteen pieces, because that is the number I aim to embroider each month. Eighteen for good luck, because eighteen means to always prosper.

The phoenixes are the most challenging. Encik Abdullah advised me to charge more for those and to embroider them on hankies as well, not just on bibs. He was right on both counts. Not every design is valued the same and I should add more variety to my goods. I raised the price for the phoenixes. And because phoenixes are worth more, I focus on my dream with every stitch that makes up this mythical and powerful bird. I want to help all mui tsai build a fire where they can emerge a triumphant phoenix.

When the time was right, I told Ah Wan Jie of my business venture.

'Ah Wan Jie, you know all that sewing I've been doing? Well, I've been selling my hankies and bibs with Encik Abdullah's help.'

But I don't mention my dream either. Ah Wan Jie was surprisingly very supportive of my business. She even said I could sew in the kitchen during the day, where the light is better. I showed her a phoenix pattern and told her that I'd decided to raise the price for them. She smiled broadly, her eyes reflecting approval.

'Ah Mei, you're doing the right thing and I'm so proud of you,' she told me over dinner, on the night before the seventh month.

Then she gave me a red paper envelope filled with money and wished me happy birthday.

'Here's a little something for your eighteenth. Consider it a gift towards your venture as well.'

* * *

Ah Wan Jie lights three red candles and sticks them into the earth next to all the food. Then, she pours some rice wine into three cups and scatters some Hell money around. She lights nine joss sticks and sticks three each into the bowls of sticky rice.

'You can go back to Number One Madam, now, Choo. No need for you to stay. It's ok, don't look so scared, you're safe, just follow the path towards the light.'

I look towards the house after throwing the last of the paper ingots into the pyre. The light, fired by electricity, shines brightly in the kitchen, a beacon calling us home. An electric light in the kitchen was Master Lee's idea.

'That's the last of the Hell money, Ah Wan Jie. We're all done?'

'Yes, Ah Mei, all done for this year's rituals. Let's leave the ghosts to enjoy their feast, shall we?' she says, making tracks to go back to the house. 'I just have one more thing to add, Mei.'

'Yes, Ah Wan Jie, what is it?' I turn to look at her. She stops walking and takes my hands in hers. She gives them a tight squeeze before speaking again.

'Mei, I didn't get to say this last night, so I'll say it now before I forget,' she says, her eyes boring into mine, looking for a way into my soul. 'A woman's freedom lies not in the man she marries—'

I nod in agreement. I know what she is going to say next. I let her have the last word.

'... but in the purse strings that she holds. Her own.'

Tugging my right hand, Ah Wan Jie pulls me along as she continues walking towards the house. The heat from the pyre is strong and I can hear the fire hissing and crackling behind us. A loud crack makes us turn around and we both gasp in unison.

Golden-yellow tongues of fire lick the evening air. They turn an electric blue before curling into a flaming red ball. A piercing squawk like a shrill scream joins the crackling. Then, a sizzling emanates from the billowing flames and a phoenix shoots out of the fire. She spirals in the air, her tail feathers sparkling and glittering. She takes flight towards the moon, leaving behind a plume of orange and red, and disappears into the sky.

Author's Note and Acknowledgements

The House of Little Sisters is a work of fiction. It is infused with historical facts, making this story a work of historical fiction. It is also a story that includes snippets of personal family lore and history. This story was written partly from memory and lived experience but mostly from research. Where there are gaps in my memory, research filled them along with a healthy dose of imagination. Any inaccuracies are my own.

While Lim Mei Mei and Hassan Mohamed are fictional, the plight of the mui tsai, indentured servant girls, was real. The physical and emotional abuse that Ah Lian and Ah Poh experience is dramatized here to reflect the reality that many girls and women lived through during the era of what the British administration termed the 'Mui Tsai Problem', and unfortunately still continue to live through today, though not always as indentured servants, but as humans trafficked to serve the needs of the wealthy, the greedy and the perverted. The stigma of rape is real. The #metoo movement is a global movement that cannot fizzle out lest we forget that women's bodies belong to them and to nobody else but them/us. So, the more we rage, the more we get heard.

Mister Pickering and Mrs Shirin Fozdar are historical figures, plucked from their timelines to inhabit the timeline of this story. I did this to pay tribute to both these people who have contributed to the Singapore narrative in so many ways.

When I started out to write this book, I wanted to explore the relationship between masters and servants in British Malaya, looking at the history of indentured servitude in China, its links to and importation into Malaya, and its impact on contemporary Singaporean and Malaysian society. As I worked on my story, I realized that my main character—Lim Mei Mei—was transformed by her love for Hassan, an Indian-Muslim boy who dreams of being a poet. This took me by surprise as I did not start out wanting to explore race relations in British Malaya or present-day Singapore and Malaysia. Without wanting to enter too much into the political space of race relations, I wrote this story to better understand the anachronistic cultural, imperialistic (and colonial) attitudes to race and to fill this story with a love that goes beyond racial constructs. When I finished the story, I realized that I did enter a political space. Race relations are political relations as long as there are people who still believe in a superior race and that inter-racial marriages or relationships are wrong. When people can be seen simply as people and not be defined by their race, then race relations will be normalized and will no longer occupy a political space. As a writer and activist for diversity and inclusion, I live in hope for that day.

The more I worked on my story and the more research I did on servants in British Malaya, the British colonies, Australia, the United States of America, China and Great Britain, I discovered that women can be both the instigator of their own oppression as well as the activist of their own freedom. Likewise, they can also be responsible for imprisoning or liberating other women. So, I invented Ah Wan Jie, a character who has internalized the patriarchy but possesses a heart of gold. Ah Wan Jie is just as imprisoned by the patriarchy as much as the men in this story (and the world) are. The Patriarchy serves nobody. I also realized that the way some societies and communities treat domestic helpers has a historical root, and that in every ten women and men who were/are employed to serve, there will be one who managed/manages to break the bonds that bind them, and this one would become the inspiration for others fighting for freedom. In history as in life, it always takes only one.

Percy Lee was born of my imagination. Like Percy, I wanted to understand how some families can be complicitous in maintaining the master/servant hierarchy, and what I can do better as someone who depends on women to help me domestically. I wrote Percy in to reveal, not confirm, what I already know about the British legal and administration system towards slavery and emancipation, and to better understand the relationship between master/mistress and servants and its socio-historical roots. I also wanted to explore the bond between the master and servant that can sometimes stretch beyond death. So, I wrote in Ah Ping Yee or Ping-chieh, the Black and White servant who brought Percy Lee up and whom he loves more than his own mother, whom he never knew, and his step-mother, Number One Madam, whom he has no emotional bond with. Ah Ping Yee or Ping-chieh, although a fictional character, was inspired by a real person. In my family, we were privileged to have had a Black and White servant who was my nanny for some years. When the winds of change blew asunder the family finances, this nanny, whom I have vague memories of being attached to, was let go. In working on this project, I have found her again.

I love poetry but am not a poet, though I aspire to be one. Rabindranath Tagore, a poet, writer, philosopher and social reformer, amongst other things, was the first non-European to win the Nobel Prize for Literature in 1913. I wanted to draw light to his poetry because when I first read one of his poems, it made me cry. I also want to pay tribute to this Bengali poet because he understood what freedom is and means. I love *Let Me Not Forget* which I share here. I prefaced the book with 'That I want thee, only thee' because this poem is timeless and captures the very essence of love.

The term 'Peranakan-Chinese' did not come into usage until the mid-1960s. According to Baba Peter Wee, a consultant of all things Peranakan, it was only after 1966 that the Straits Chinese became referred to as Peranakan-Chinese. Before that they were known as Baba-Nyonya, a compound noun made up of two Portuguese words: *baba*, meaning father, and *nona*, meaning woman or grandmother. The Peranakan-Chinese are also known by the term Straits Chinese, though the latter include ethnic Chinese born in the Straits of Malacca. Many Peranakan-Chinese were educated in English with the aim of working in British civil service. Some were court interpreters, like my great-grandfather or petition writers, like my grandfather. For their contribution to the British administration under King George VI, the Peranakan-Chinese were also referred to as the King's Chinese. I have chosen to use Peranakan-Chinese as an identity marker in my story because that is how I see myself.

I hope that this story would inspire young readers to find out more, amongst other things, about the history of indentured servitude and seek ways to advocate for more empathy and compassion towards the many who have had to leave their homes to work in other people's homes. Although this story is categorized as Young Adult (YA), the readership can also cross over to adult. I have a deep belief that adults who read have children who will read. I have every confidence that this is how stories are passed down.

This novel brings up some challenging issues that many young adults and adults face. If you have found them to be triggering, please seek help by asking a teacher, parent or counsellor for advice. There are helplines that you can call. I list them at the end of the book. Please know that you are not alone and that there is always help at the end of the line.

The places where I did my research were the National Library of Singapore, the National Archives (Singapore), The National Archives and The British Library. While I do not know the following individuals personally, their work, research and lives informed my story. I was fortunate to discover Dr Sandy Chang's research on gender, intimacy and Chinese migration in British Malaya. Excerpts of her work have been particularly helpful in filling the gaps of research in regard to female servants in and Chinese migration to British Malaya. Her grant proposal, which can be found online and an interview she gave in Malaysia added to my own research and brought more texture and layers to the story. Dr Rachel Leow's paper, '*Do you own non-Chinese mui tsai?*' *Re-examining Race and Female Servitude in Malaya and Hong Kong, 1919–1939* (Modern Asian Studies, Vol. 46, No. 6, November 2012, Cambridge University Press), has been particularly helpful to this project in helping me understand that the trading of mui tsai, a Chinese phenomenon, did not only occur within the Chinese community in British Malaya, and that not all mui tsai were Chinese. Indentured servitude is a global phenomenon and is still in existence today, albeit in variegated and disguised forms. The late Janet Lim Chiu Mei's personal story as a mui tsai who escaped servitude and survived the Second World War to become the first nurse from Singapore to study nursing in Great Britain has been an inspiration. Her autobiography *Sold for Silver* opened my eyes to a lived experience that research could not reflect.

I write about food a lot because food is central to all human experience. Food is what brings people together and is always a symbol of friendship and love. As a former food blogger, it gives me no end of pleasure to talk about food, to describe the mouthfeel of each dish, and the textures and tastes of every mouthful. Writing about food requires the writer to experience each dish through their five senses and memory. As a Peranakan-Chinese, rempahs, sambals and chillies are central to my family's kitchen. There are many Peranakan dishes that are quickly vanishing, like babi tohay. I conjured this dish up, thanks to the help of Tham Kah Whai, an enthusiast of all things Peranakan, and Malcolm Lee, the head chef at Candlenut, Singapore's only one Michelin Star Peranakan restaurant. The roti John and its invention is relatively undocumented. It is said that roti John was invented in the 1970s when an American sailor asked a South Asian hawker in Singapore to make him a hamburger. Roti John is also found in Malaysia, and is known as the Asian hamburger. I think it is a very good example of 'East meets West' and is a unique marker of a Malayan identity. Food as a cultural and identity marker is not unique to Singapore and Malaysia. As a hybrid cuisine, Peranakan-Chinese dishes combine a rich array of recipes that can be considered an appropriation and appreciation of Malay ingredients and dishes. It is a fusion of ancient Chinese recipes and indigenous Malay ones giving the Peranakan table a unique aesthetic and flavour. I want to pay homage to my great grandmother, who was a nyonya and someone whom I know through my father's stories. I want to pay tribute to my mother who, being a sinkeh—an ethnic Chinese—adopted and adapted the Peranakan cuisine when she married my father. It is because of my mum that our meals are colourful pots of reds, oranges and ochres. Adopting, adapting and assimilating is what every diaspora community knows well. For a history on the Malay cuisine and table, read *The Food of Singapore Malays: Gastronomic Travels Through the Archipelago* by Khir Johari. There are several Peranakan-Chinese cookbooks available. I have no favourites as they are all comparably good.

My research also included folklore and fairytales, particularly those of East and Southeast Asian traditions. My thanks go to Jennifer Wong for her nuggets of inspiration. I am indebted to Sarah Leipciger, Jess Lowe, Anastasia Odu, Ellis Saxey, Polly Foster and Erica Duggan who read the drafts of this book so diligently and carefully. A writer's craft is dependent on so many things, and being part of a supportive critique group is one of them. Thanks also go to Joyce Chng who is the inspiration behind my search for Southeast Asian folklore. I must mention Zakir Hossain Khokan, a prize-winning Bangladeshi writer, poet and activist for inclusion and diversity. Zakir is a construction quality controller and his activism in making the migrant workers of Singapore be seen and heard is beyond description. He is the founder of the writing group, *Migrant Writers of Singapore* and the curator of the visual arts festival, *Migrant Worker Photography Festival*, which showcases works of art by migrant workers. Zakir's *One Bag One Book* initiative to get migrant workers to read more and carry at least one book in their bag wherever they go moved me to tears. Zakir was the inspiration for Hassan. I met Zakir through June Ho, who is also an activist in getting people to read more. June is the founder of the No Bull Channel where she talks about books and the importance of reading.

I am grateful to my family—mum and dad and my sisters— for their love, support and encouragement. I'm especially indebted to my dad who never tires of telling me stories about his youth, growing up in British Malaya in the early '30s, '40s and '50s. Both my parents grew up as British subjects in Malaya, Daddy in Malaysia, Mummy in Singapore, to both becoming independent citizens of the Republic of Singapore. As overseas Chinese, they continue to forge an identity that is uniquely called the Chinese diaspora. I am immensely thankful to my husband, Armando Nava and daughters, Sophie Stretch and Raffaella Nava—my rock and jewels—who have been patient as I talk through my story with them at the dinner table, where conversations are always lively and spiced with anecdotes and memories. As people of the diaspora, my husband and daughters know only too well what drives me as a Singapore-born British East and Southeast Asian to write the stories that I do. I would like to extend my thanks to Nora Abu Bakar, who believed in this story, and to my agent, Lydia Silver, whom I met after agreeing to work on this project for Penguin SEA—you've been wonderfully supportive. Much thanks also go to the editing team at Penguin Random House for their eye to detail and constructive feedback. I would like to thank Thatchaayanie Renganathan, in particular, for her astute eye to detail and diligent structural editing of this novel.

Every story has a right of place in history and should be told for posterity. I hope that this story has given aspiring children's writers in Southeast Asia some inspiration to pen more stories that keep our history and culture alive, lest the children who come after us forget.

Eva Wong Nava
London, 2021.

Book Club Questions

1. The novel started with a different title, before it was changed to *The House of The Little Sisters,* what do you think the title could have been previously? Why do you think the editor changed the title? [hint: it included the name of a heritage food.]

2. What do you think of the current title? Do you think it reflects the themes in the novel?

3. (a) Which character did you relate to the most, and why? (b) What chapter or scenes resonated with you the most, and why?

4. What were Ah Wan Jie's motivations throughout the novel? Explain why you felt this way.

5. Critiques have said that Ah Mei could have done more, do you agree? (a) What more could Ah Mei have done? (b) If you were in Ah Mei's shoes, what would you have done?

6. Before reading *The House of the Little Sisters* did you know about the Mui Tsai Ordinance of 1932? Does the novel inspire you to want to learn more about the Mui Tsai Problem in British Malaya? What do you understand about indentured servitude?

7. Why did the author choose to write in the character of Shirin Fozdar? Have you heard of Shirin Fozdar before reading this novel? Do you think that Shirin Fozdar is a feminist, and why? What does feminism mean to you?

8. Some readers have commented on the character of Percy Lee, speculating that he could have been in love with Ah Mei—were there any parts in the novel where you felt this way? What is the significance of Percy Lee's character in the story?

9. Are you convinced by Hassan's love for Ah Mei? How do you think their relationship would have developed? Do you think that as a couple Ah Mei and Hassan have a future together, given the setting?

10. How did you feel about the novel's ending? What do the symbolisms at the end mean to you? How would you change the ending if you could change it?

11. This is considered an Own Voices story. What do you think #ownvoices is about?

12. Bonus question: Who do you think the man with the glass eye is, and why?